THE ILLUSIONIST

THE ILLUSIONIST

Jennifer Johnston

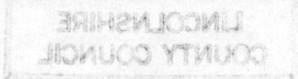

C

CHIVERS LARGE PRINT
BATH

British Library Cataloguing in Publication Data available

This Large Print edition published by Chivers Press, Bath, 1997.

Published by arrangement with Reed Consumer Books Ltd.

U.K. Hardcover ISBN 0 7451 8818 4
U.K. Softcover ISBN 0 7451 8819 2

Photoset, printed and bound in Great Britain by
Redwood Books, Trowbridge, Wiltshire

*This book is for Fanny,
with love and gratitude
for many years of
friendship*

I sit in a room full of light and shade.

I dream.

I dream of her entrance.

She will come into the room as if she were coming onto a stage, or anyway that's the way I see it from where I sit, from where I think about it.

A fire burns in the grate. From time to time it spits sparks onto the hearthrug and I make a mental note to chastise the man with the horse and cart from whom I bought the neatly chopped logs of wood when next I see him.

There are trees outside the window, just coming into leaf and the light in the room is filtered through the acid green of newly born leaves. A bright, cold light.

I imagine she will be dressed in black.

Smart. She always looks smart. Short skirts when fashion demands it; long skirts, but not too long, at other times. Her face will be pale, but quite controlled. I haven't known her to cry since she was a child. To be quite honest, I have hardly known her since she was a child.

'I didn't think people wore black to funerals these days.'

That's what I will say to her. After I have kissed her of course.

Kissed her pale cold face.

1

Maybe she will smile slightly.

'You can suit yourself really. It's up to you.'

'Like hats. No one wears a hat to church any longer, so I'm told ... except for your grandmother, of course. Most other old ladies go bareheaded these days. So I'm told.'

'As I said, it's up to you.'

'Were there many people there?'

She will look past me, out of the window. She will not reply.

'A good crowd? I do hope there was a good crowd.'

'Quite a good crowd.'

I won't know whether to believe her or not.

'Anyone I would know?'

She will shrug. Again she will not reply.

'I don't suppose so, after all these years. Except for Dr Rhodes and Peter Magill. Were they there? Old. They'd be quite old now.'

I won't ask about women. That might not be appropriate.

'I wonder if he'll rise from the grave. I bet he'll try. I do hope that is one trick he hasn't mastered. You'd never know with him. Would you?'

'What about a cup of tea?'

'Perhaps you should have had him cremated.'

'Tea, Mother.'

'I'm sorry. I shouldn't say things like that.'

'You always did though.'

'Let's have tea.'

2

*   *   *

A somewhat splenetic dream or vision perhaps.

Maybe before I launch into this sliver of a tale, I should explain myself, pass the time until she arrives to make her entrance backstage right.

I am a writer.

I have been writing novels for the last fifteen years or so, with varying degrees of success. Well, let's say I have a door and I keep the wolf from it.

It is important for the self-esteem not to have to beg, borrow or steal.

One of the long windows behind my back is half open and the curtains tremble in the spring breeze. I always sit with my back to the window when I work. I like to have the light falling over my shoulder onto the page, almost green light, as today, or the pale grey of city light, which is the most usual and sometimes in the early morning a streak of gold will reach this room and will enliven my hands on the keyboard and paper in front of me. Also, I like to face the door as I work, so that I cannot be taken too much by surprise. I have never really enjoyed surprises.

Now, I sit here and dream of a meeting that will take place between myself and my daughter in the not too distant future.

There is never silence in this room, in spite of

3

the protecting trees; the constant hum of the city comforts me. Voices in the street, the distant slamming of doors, the cars that splash past on wet nights, the moan on autumn evenings of the fog-horns that surround Dublin Bay, all these familiar sounds keep me warm.

I live alone.

Sometimes people commiserate with me, talk about loneliness, the prospect of old age alone, the emptiness of a solitary life. I let them ramble on. I smile and nod my head.

'I'm sure you're right,' I say from time to time. That makes them happy and we change the subject.

I like to be able to close the door on the world, dress, undress when I feel like it; eat, fast, read, write, dance, sing, talk to the wall, talk to myself.

'Talking to yourself is the first sign of madness.'

How often did Martyn say that to me?

I made sure he never caught me dancing in the kitchen when I should have been stirring the white sauce, or foxtrotting with the hoover.

There were certain tunes I found irresistible … still do … 'Puttin' on the Ritz', for example, or 'It's Only a Paper Moon'.

A bit old-fashioned, but a good dancing beat.

Irresistible.

Martyn couldn't dance.

4

Perhaps he just didn't want to dance.

He had such control, such flexibility of his limbs that I am sure he could have danced if he had wanted to.

Maybe in one of his other lives he dazzled on the dance floor.

Who knows!

Even now after all these years I sometimes have the same dream about him. A strong, strange dream, always the same.

He stands in the dark, slightly above me, his arms outstretched, weighted down almost with the white doves.

He stands quite still.

The birds move uneasily at first, clamping with their claws on the sleeves and shoulders of his black silk jacket.

He is quite unperturbed by their agitation.

They drift down through the darkness like huge snowflakes and land on his sleeves and his shoulders.

He stands quite still and after a while the birds settle into an almost drowsy torpor, no murmurs, no fidgeting.

Quite, quite still.

At this point of stillness he begins to move his arms, slowly up and down, up and down.

The wings tremble.

Up and down.

And soon they move rhythmically with the movement of his arms.

Up and down.

Deep, sweeping strokes, and the man is transformed into an angel with heavy, white wings beating as he hovers above the darkness of the world.

I always struggle to wake up at this moment, afraid. I suppose ... though it is only in recent days that I have discovered what I was afraid of ... that he might dissolve into some hail of feathers in which I might drown.

I hope I will never have this dream again.

The daughter for whom I wait is called Robin.

An odd name for a woman.

He chose the name.

He chose everything that happened in the life he spent with me.

I think he saw her as a little brown bird in the first few weeks of her life. Her warm head throbbed in his hands like the heart of a bird when you find it imprisoned in a room and catch it in your hands in order to release it out into freedom again.

Her real names, you know, the ones for passports and other official purposes, are Emily Marion, chosen also by him; a pair of unused names, like a pair of old shoes gathering dust under a bed or in the back of a cupboard. Unwanted.

Who wants someone's discarded shoes?

Who wants someone's discarded names?

I am Stella.

I have worn that name quite well for fifty-eight years.

I quite enjoy it.

He called me Star. I must say that for a while I also quite enjoyed that intimacy.

*   *   *

I suppose I wasn't much of a mother.

Fair to average would be a reasonable assessment.

She was always her father's girl; his Robin.

He was confident of her love. I was always too anxious; I tried to remember too much how it had been when I was a child, the things that had troubled me, the things that had pleased me; the darknesses of childhood and the wild joys.

Maybe he had no childhood to remember, that was always the impression that he gave, a man whose life was wholly in the future, unrolling in front of him like some brand-new motorway.

Robin has never forgiven me for leaving him and I'm sure that her conversations with me over the next day or so will be peppered with mildly recriminatory comments. I will endeavour to keep my lip buttoned.

My mother, on the other hand, saw through Martyn like a pane of glass.

She met him first when she and my father were over, spending a few days with me in London.

7

I had known Martyn at that stage for about six months and was obviously to my mother's eyes in the process of losing my wits.

'Why does he spell his name with a Y?' she asked, the morning after he had dropped in casually for a drink.

She was eating toast. My father was still in the bathroom and I could hear my somewhat unreliable gas geyser roaring down the passage.

'Why?' she repeated.

She has a special way of eating toast, no crusts of course, and the toast cut into neat triangles. She loads the butter and then the marmalade onto one tip of the triangle and then ... snap. As she chews she loads the next tip, ready for the next snap. She still has her own snapping teeth and absolutely no fear of cholesterol, sugar, alcohol, cigarette smoke or any of those other horrors that keep all the rest of us uneasily on the tightrope.

The geyser subsided slowly into silence.

'I don't know, Mother. I've never asked him.'

'Well you should. I always think it's important to know why people do things.'

'It's a free world. Anyone can spell their name the way they wish.'

Snap.

'I hope Father's got enough hot water.'

'I have never heard of anyone spelling Martin with a Y.'

8

'Well, now you have.'

Snap.

'Will he come to the theatre with us this evening?'

I shook my head.

'He doesn't like the theatre.'

'I do hope you know what you're doing.'

Snap.

*   *   *

A different tree grew outside my window then. A lilac, with deep purple flowers that scented the room on warm spring evenings.

Lilacs like lime.

Lilacs prefer London to Dublin.

It's to do with the lime.

At that time I was preferring London to Dublin.

It was to do with my mother.

I don't mean to be unkind, but at that stage of my life I had to find things out for myself, discover courage, make mistakes. She always found it quite difficult to let me do any of these things. She believed in grammar, not just the grammar of language, but also that of behaviour in both public and private living. She believed in God. She believed that woman's power existed only as far as she could manipulate men.

I had trouble with all those beliefs, so I preferred my anonymity in London.

9

'Glover,' she said, considering the name.

It meant nothing to her.

It rang no bells in her head.

She snapped the last piece of toast into her mouth.

My father came into the room at that moment and the inquisition stopped before it had really begun.

At some later time she said to me:

'I must say, I can't see you married to a conjuror.'

'An illusionist, Mother,' I corrected her. 'A part-time illusionist.'

'Isn't it one and the same?'

'No, it's not. He doesn't take rabbits out of hats at children's parties.'

She sniffed.

'Well? What does he do?'

'He creates illusions.' At this time I was on shaky ground, as I had only his word for it. 'Rather a splendid thing to do, don't you think?'

She made no reply.

'Illusion. Magic. The stuff dreams are made of.'

We were standing by the window, way down below us the sea sparkled savagely, from this room in their house you could see no other buildings, just the sea in all its moods.

'You shouldn't use such fanciful words

10

about him. The man is a part-time conjuror. He has charm all right. I can see that. Think more than twice dear. If you want to throw yourself away on some unexplained man who calls himself Martyn, that's your affair. But don't say...' She stopped.

'Don't say what?'

She sighed.

'Nothing, darling. Nothing. Your father and I just want you to be happy.'

*   *   *

I am attempting to tell a story. Starting at the tail end is part of my writer's bag of tricks. I suppose I could call myself an illusionist also, except for the fact that he has already bagged that title.

It is a long, slithery sliver of a tale, that came to a sticky end the other day, a cold, windy autumn day in London.

Perhaps it was the sort of end he would have wished; here one minute and gone the next. A sleight-of-hand ending to his invented life.

An IRA bomb in a London street and Martyn in his station wagon with a hundred and fifty white doves neatly caged in the back.

I think at this moment of the demolished doves, the feathers drifting down like snowflakes from the evening sky, falling on the wreckage of cars and shattered glass and the frightened injured and dead Martyn. Everyone

11

at the wrong place at the wrong time. I hope they felt nothing at that last moment, no pain, no anxiety.

This morning he was buried in London and I am waiting for our daughter to arrive. I will console her if I can, though I doubt that she will reveal the extent of her pain to me. She will not stay long. She feels ill at ease in Dublin. She speaks with an alien voice, looks at the city with the critical eye of a stranger.

I love her, but doubt whether she cares.

*　　　*　　　*

When I read I become lost to this world. For moments after I lift my eyes from the page I find it hard to refocus on reality. I see the landscape of fiction around me, hear in my head the voices of the writer's imagination. So, when almost thirty years ago, the man sitting opposite to me in the train from Liverpool to Euston plucked the book from my hands, I was taken aback. I had been quite unaware of his presence in the compartment with me. I had been quite unaware of the landmarks already passed on my journey. Had I passed Chester? Crewe? Rugby?

'Hey,' I said.

He sat back in his seat smiling at me, my book in his hand.

Slag heaps rocked past the window.

'Good morning.'

12

Voice melodious, not Irish, possibly Welsh, I thought.

'You'll be blind before you're forty if you read so much. Or mad.'

'When I want your advice I'll ask for it.'

'I'd like that, really, I would.'

'In the meantime, please may I have my book back?'

Carefully he put the book down on the seat beside him.

Still slag hills, no green and pleasant land outside the windows.

He leant towards me slowly, gently stretching out one hand and took an egg from my ear.

'See!'

He held it up in front of my eyes, carefully balanced between the first finger and thumb of his right hand.

A smattering of raindrops smacked against the window of the train; the sky was now as grey as the slag heaps.

He shook his fingers in a somewhat fastidious way and the egg disappeared.

I began to laugh.

For a moment he allowed me to laugh on my own, then he joined in.

He laughed because he was pleased with his performance, pleased also with my laughter.

He shook his head from side to side as he laughed, but watched me always, gripped me with his eyes.

13

I felt light-hearted.

I always feel warmed by people who can laugh at their own absurdities as well as those of the world.

When my laughter tailed away, I wondered what would happen next.

Was the joke over?

He held his hands out toward me across the table, empty hands, palms up, white, slender hands, bony fingers, bony wrists. He flipped his hands over and I looked at the bones, the blue veins under the skin. His nails were neat, well clipped. A gold watch on his left wrist seemed almost too heavy for him.

'Would you like a cup of coffee?'

His voice was polite, formal.

'What a lot of equipment you must carry up your sleeves.'

'Well ... actually...'

His hands moved. Rather self-consciously he touched each cuff in turn.

'... I have a thermos in my ...'

He indicated a small case above him in the rack with a movement of his eyes.

'I'd love one. Thank you.'

He got up and pulled the case down from the rack. He opened it and took out a thermos flask and a small plastic cup which he put on the table.

'Sugar?'

I shook my head.

He fastened the case again and replaced it on

14

the rack.

He sat down and unscrewed the top of the flask. He placed it on the table by the cup. All his movements were neat and ordered.

'I'm afraid there's milk in it.'

'That's fine by me.'

'I always put milk in it.'

'I'm sure it's much better than anything British Rail could produce.'

He carefully filled the cup and pushed it over towards me and then filled the flask top for himself.

'Thanks.'

The train rocked as I raised the cup to my lips and the coffee swirled dangerously, but didn't quite spill.

'Delicious,' I said.

He stared at me with a faint smile on his face.

Steam from the two cups drifted between us.

There was something about his smile that made me nervous.

'Charles Martyn Glover,' he said. 'Commonly known as Martyn. M.A.R.T.Y.N.'

'Why not Charles?'

'Forget Charles. What about you?'

'Me?'

'Your name? Names?'

'Oh, yes.'

For a moment I couldn't remember. I dipped my head towards the coffee cup and closed my eyes in the hope that a miracle would

15

occur. The smell of coffee did the trick.

'Stella Macnamara.'

I kept my eyes closed as I said my name.

'Oirish?'

I opened my eyes and looked at him.

'You don't sound Oirish.'

I didn't bother to reply.

The slag heaps had given way to neatly hedged fields.

The train shuddered and then slowly stopped, brakes grinding onto wheels, smoke and sparks belched over the green fields.

My coffee splashed out of the cup and over the sleeve of my coat.

'Oh, damn.'

'Allow me.'

His hand offered me a large white folded handkerchief.

'I couldn't possibly ... I have one somewhere...'

He shook the handkerchief at me and I took it and mopped at myself.

'Thank you.'

I shoved the stained handkerchief across the table towards him. He let it lie there untouched as he stared out through the window.

'Sunday,' he said eventually, picking up the handkerchief and rolling it into a little ball. 'They mend the lines on Sunday. I always say to myself, never travel on a Sunday, but here I am. Luckily.' He bowed gallantly towards me.

'Yes.'

16

'We could be stranded here for half an hour, or more.'

'Yes.'

'Like to play a game of cards?'

He produced a pack of cards and riffled them through the air.

I though with a sudden panic of all the stories I had heard of naïve passengers in trains being lured into playing cards with innocent-seeming strangers.

'Ah, no thank you.'

He riffled, fanned, shuffled. The cards flew like birds through the air. He smiled slightly as he watched them fly.

'May I have my book back, please?'

He caught all the cards in his right hand as he stretched out with his left and picked up my book. He placed it on the table in front of me.

'Thank you.'

I found my place and began to read.

I can't remember what book it was.

I might, at that time, have been going through my French phase.

It could have been Camus, Sartre, Nathalie Sarraute, Marguerite Duras. Could have been.

Cold, winter day 1961.

Could have been any one of those.

Could, on the other hand, have been Agatha Christie.

Whatever it was, I drew the words around me like a stockade.

The carriage trembled with occasional

17

buffets of wind and the raindrops streaming down the windows hid the landscape.

The heating pipes by my right ankle ticked and sighed and gave out very little warmth.

He sighed on the other side of the table.

I heard him reassemble the thermos flask and put it away in his case.

He tapped the cards together on the table, ordering them, and then put them into their box.

He coughed.

He refolded the handkerchief that he had lent me and then he sighed again.

With a jolt or two and a long, sad scream the train began to creep once more along the tracks.

I took my eyes from my book and looked out of the window.

Six men leaned on shovels by the side of the track, watching us go by.

One of them waved at me.

I smiled; a smile he probably never saw.

Cautiously I looked across the table.

He appeared to be asleep, his head leaning sideways into the corner, his mouth slightly open.

He was handsome all right, even in sleep with his mouth slightly open. A bit flash perhaps.

He opened his eyes and stared at me.

I felt my face go red.

I dropped my eyes to my book.

18

We clattered into Euston about an hour late.

The ran had stopped and it was bitterly cold.

Even though it was only early afternoon, the air was dusk coloured.

'Allow me. Oh do allow me.'

He pulled my case from my hand and swung it down onto the platform.

Steam drifted up from under the train.

I thought of poor old Celia Johnson in that terrible hat. I thought of Anna Karenina.

The engine made a yawning noise as we walked past it. I knew how it felt.

He was speaking to me.

'Where are you heading for?'

'Notting Hill. I have a ... Notting Hill.'

'Great,' he said. 'I can give you a lift in my cab.'

He began to stride out through the shuffling crowd.

'You needn't bother. I ...'

I had to hurry to keep up with him.

He walked with his head hunched down into his shoulders to keep warm. He walked to the head of the taxi queue and opened the door of the taxi that was drifting slowly along the kerb. He jumped in with the case and then held out his hand to me.

'Hey you!'

He slammed the door shut in the face of a furious protester.

19

'Notting Hill,' he said to the driver and then turned and grinned at me.

'You shouldn't have done that. There's a queue.'

'I hate queues. I never stand in queues. We could have been standing there for half an hour with all those orderly people.'

'I am an orderly person.'

'I think you are just afraid of disorder. I can see it in your face. Those people out there are just sheep.'

London was greasy and dour and I was glad that I didn't have to stand for half an hour in a bleak queue.

Winter Sunday afternoon, the street lights hanging sadly in the rain. Those people who were out seemed grey like the air as they hurried beneath their umbrellas to walk their dogs or make their Sunday duty visits.

'Where do you live?'

'Chalk Farm.'

'You are going a long way round.'

'I chose to.'

'Are you a conjuror?'

'An illusionist.'

'I'm sorry.'

'Not professionally. I just have this great interest. Always have. And a facility. I have very good hands.'

He spread them out on his knees and looked at them with pride.

'I don't take rabbits out of hats at children's

parties. Illusionist is the word, for future reference.'

'I'll remember that. But you must admit that taking eggs out of people's ears is pretty run-of-the-mill stuff.'

'There's not much you can do in trains. Unexpectedly. Just a few basic tricks. Any fool can do that sort of thing.'

He held his right hand out toward me, flicked it in the air for a moment, spread his fingers wide and presented me with a red silk handkerchief.

I took it from him and looked at it. A nice cheerful colour, good quality silk.

'Jolly good.'

I handed it back to him.

He waved his hand.

'It's a present.'

'Really, I...'

'Don't argue, woman, keep it. There are plenty more where that came from.'

The driver pushed the window open.

'Whereabouts in Notting Hill, sir?'

I leant forward towards him, the silk cloth crumpled in my hand.

'Turn left into Holland Park and then immediately right. It's the right-hand corner house.'

I turned to Martyn, in case he thought I lived in some sort of grandeur.

'I have half a basement...'

'Have you a telephone?'

21

I ignored that.

'Half a basement. A bit dark in the winter, but very nice. I have two big rooms. K and B.'

I sounded like an *Evening Standard* advertisement.

'Constant hot water and central heating.'

I looked at him.

In the flickering light from the street lamps his face looked like a flickering character from an old movie. No emotion, flick, stony, Jimmy Cagney, flick flick, Herbert Lom, George Raft. Serious villains, every one.

I wanted to laugh, but thought he mightn't be amused.

'All mod cons,' I said instead. 'The lap of luxury.'

'Yes.'

He turned and smiled at me as he spoke. It was a warm and friendly smile, almost loving.

'Oh God,' I thought.

The taxi lurched to the left and then immediately to the right and stopped.

'Well, here we are.'

I fumbled in my bag.

'Don't be daft,' he said, putting a hand on mine.

I got quickly out into the bitter air and pulled my case after me. I put the case on the pavement and held my hand out towards him.

He leaned out from the taxi and kissed the palm of my hand, folded the fingers over and handed it back to me.

After the taxi had driven off, splattering greasy mud as it went, I realised that I had packed my hall door key in the bottom of my suitcase.

* * *

The recollection of that disorderly moment makes me smile.

I never learnt to be orderly, much as I thought I wanted to.

My mother always wears gloves when she goes out in the street.

Once when I went up to her room to fetch something for her I found twenty pairs of gloves in a drawer.

I counted them.

Palm to palm; leather, suede, pigskin, cotton, black, brown, blue.

Palm to palm.

A drawer full of praying gloves.

Or, I suppose, kissing.

Good quality.

Things must last.

Care, polish, cherish.

For ever.

I suppose she has a point of view.

She never thought Martyn was good quality.

* * *

The doorbell rings.

A short buzz and then a longer one.

23

It will be Robin.

I get up and go to let her in.

She is not wearing black.

She doesn't have a suitcase, just a soft leather bag slung over her shoulder. Her face is pale, her eyes hidden by dark glasses, which she doesn't remove when I open the door.

'Oh, darling,' I say, holding out my arms to her.

She touches my cheek with her cold cheek and comes past me into the hall.

She takes off her coat and throws it onto a chair.

'God, I'm tired. I came straight from the cemetery. It was so cold at the graveside I thought all my faculties would freeze up. That bloody taxi driver robbed me. Twenty quid he charged me to come here.'

'They're notorious at the airport. Go in and sit down by the fire and I'll make a cup of tea.'

'Gin and tonic, large, no lemon. I mean to say, Star, Mother, Mum, forget the tea at a time like this.'

She moves across the hall, trailing behind her the soft bag.

I go into the kitchen and think about my scenario as I get her drink and a glass of wine for myself. I decide against using any part of it.

She is hunched into an armchair, staring into the fire.

She takes the glass from my hand without looking at me.

24

'Thanks.'

I sit down opposite her.

'I don't want to talk just at the moment,' she says, 'I just want to sit here and thaw out. So just let me.'

I nod. I lean back into my chair and look at her tense figure.

'Fuck bloody Martyn,' I think.

*   *   *

The scent of smoke drifted from the piles of smouldering leaves. A slight mist rose with the smoke from the damp grass. The trees, chestnut, sycamore, plane, were quite still and spectral, lit by the glow of intermittent gas lights.

We were walking from my flat over Camden Hill to have dinner in some trattoria off Kensington High Street.

Mario, Nino, Luigi, Franco.

'*Rus in urbe,*' he had just said.

'This is the best time to be at home. Home, Dublin, Ireland.'

I suddenly loved the way those three words sounded, the way they fitted into my mouth, loved the way they hung in the misty air.

'We'll go tomorrow.'

'I didn't mean that . . .'

'Of course you did. I know you. Nothing you say is without meaning. We'll take an afternoon plane. I'll get Angela to arrange it in the morning.'

Angela was his secretary.

'We can't just...'

'Mattie, Mattie, Mattie.' From an open gate someone was calling his dog.

'Of course we can. I need a break. You want to go. I'd like to meet your parents again.'

'Mattie.'

'It's important, don't you think, to grasp the hour?'

'I...'

'A short autumn break. Can we stay with your parents or would it be more seemly...'

'Mattie if you don't come here now, now. I'll break your bloody neck.'

'... to stay in a hotel?'

'I'm working.'

He took my hand and held it to his lips.

'I love you Star. I want to go and see your home and your nice parents. I want to see leprechauns and drink Guinness and be charmed. Will I be charmed?'

'Maaaatie!'

'We'll pick up a car at the airport. I presume they have cars in Ireland.'

'Silly.'

'I even presume they have airports.'

The man at the gate, now some way behind us, whistled a few shrill notes.

'I don't like flying.'

'You will like it with me. You will be safe with me. Look.'

He let go of my hand and ran a few steps from me, out of the circle of the shivering light.

He looked a little absurd, I thought, as he ran in his grey flannel suit. His hands fluttered for a moment and gleamed in the light and then suddenly he seemed to be flying through the darkness of the trees. I could see his pale face and hands as he soared for a moment and then a small black-and-white dog broke from the undergrowth and ran past me up the hill.

'Good girl. Good old girl.' The voice was relieved and welcoming.

Martyn, grounded, strolled across the grass towards me.

'Flying is no problem,' he said.

'OK. You win.'

* * *

I telephoned my mother later that night, when I was alone once more in my flat.

'Do you realise what time it is?'

'It's only just after eleven. I'm sorry, I didn't ...'

'Twenty past to be exact. Is something the matter?'

I imagined her sitting up in bed, her long hair floating down over the white shawl that kept the autumn draughts from her shoulders.

She had beautiful, thick hair that she had allowed me to brush when I was a child, with her Mason Pearson pure bristle hairbrush. Long firm strokes from crown to tip which on cold days generated sparks and little cracking noises that prickled in my fingers. It was one of

27

the boys to brush her hair.

'Well?'

She sounded impatient.

'I thought we might come over for a couple of days. If it suits you, of course.'

'We?'

'Martyn and I.'

There was a pause and she said something that I couldn't hear to my father.

'When?'

'Well . . . tomorrow, if that . . .'

'Tomorrow? Really, Stella, you might have given us a little notice.'

'We only just thought of the idea this evening.'

'I'd no idea you were still seeing the conjuror.'

'Illusionist.'

'You're not going to spring any surprises on us?'

'If it doesn't suit you we can stay in an hotel.'

'Don't be silly, dear. You can perfectly well stay here.'

'We're picking up a car at the airport, so we'll . . .'

'In separate rooms, dear. You do of course understand that.'

'Mother . . .'

'I don't want anything . . . you know . . . going on. You have to think of Molly.'

Molly had been their housekeeper since their marriage thirty-four years earlier. She was the

28

repository of all our secrets. She knew more
about my life and that of my brothers than
either of our parents were ever likely to know.

'An hotel . . .'

'Sometimes, dear, you can be very childish.
You can do what you like in London, but over
here you have to think of other people's
feelings. Your father and I don't mind what
you do, but you must consider Molly . . . and
others of course. Don's children, people . . .
People.

'Your father wants to know does he play
golf?'

'I don't know.'

'Martyn who, by the way?'

'Glover.'

'Ah yes, Glover. Don't arrive till after lunch
dear. We're looking forward so much to seeing
you. Good-night.'

Thirty years back. Thereabouts.
She still had long, thick hair.
Before marriage.
Before Robin.
Before anger.

Out beyond Clifden the world seems to end:
hills, islands, clouds drift together in the huge
ocean of the sky. Sometimes the sun
overwhelms both the sea and the sky with its
glitter, sometimes pillars of rain move across
the emptiness, then the colour, the texture of

the land and sea change as the rain falls, from blue to grey, sometimes to black. Other times a shawl of mist hides mountains, sea and sky.

That day the sun was shining as we drove up the Sky road.

He drew over to the edge of the road and stopped the car. He got out and stood on the grass at the very edge where the land falls away beneath you. Wind pulled at his clothes. I got out and stood beside him.

'Now if we could fly.'

He took my hand as he spoke and for a moment I thought he was going to launch us both into space . . .

'I think we should get married, don't you? I think you are the woman I'd like to spend my life with. I should have asked you weeks ago . . . on that train perhaps, but I was afraid you might say no. If I could fly now, we could just set off together.'

He nodded his head towards the west.

'What's over there? That's where we would go.'

'America,' I said.

He laughed.

'Well? What do you say? Will we get married?'

'I thought you'd never ask.'

He pulled his hand away from mine and clapped loudly.

A startled rabbit scuttered over the short grass.

'Tell me something.'

He stopped clapping and looked at me.

'Do you love me?'

'Oh Star, silly Star, that you could ask such a question.'

It wasn't really an answer, but I didn't notice at the time.

He walked round the car and got in.

He banged the door. He sat staring out at the sky.

I wondered if I loved him.

I wondered what love was.

Need?

The body's urges?

Comforting recognitions?

Two fishing boats moved out in the distance. They must have been laden, as a crowd of gulls moved over them. The wind tangled my hair and I longed to stay in that spot for ever.

Sacrifice: so many people thought sacrifice was an integral part of love.

I thought of my parents: their absurdities, their strengths, the Ordnance Survey map of their contented lives.

The shadow of a cloud floated in the sea, beneath the boats, beneath the birds.

What did I know about them, except that they were my parents?

We were accustomed to each other.

Was that love? Or what?

He tooted the horn.

I turned and looked at him sitting there, one

hand on the horn, one elbow half out of the window.

I opened the door and got in beside him.

'Let's do it,' I sang to him. 'Let's fall in love.'

'I take it that means yes.'

'Let's do it . . .'

I leant towards him. He pulled me tight against him and kissed me. That was such a kissing . . . Thinking was blotted out. The sky, the sea and the floating boats were blotted out.

He didn't play golf, but none the less my father tried his hardest to get to know him. There were good cigars, a bottle or two of vintage port. They talked money and the law, horse racing, their heads each evening wreathed in blue smoke, politics, the stock market and power.

'He doesn't tell you anything, does he?'

My mother had come into my room as I was getting ready for dinner on our last evening in Dublin. She stood by the window, looking down into the garden. The leaves had been neatly raked into piles ready for burning the next day.

'What on earth do you want him to tell you?'

'Oh . . . you know . . . things. We'll have no chrysanthemums for Christmas if Jerry doesn't bring those plants into the greenhouse soon. He keeps his lip well buttoned.'

'Curiosity killed the cat.'

'Not always, dear.'

'I'm sorry you don't like him.'

32

'I never said I didn't like him. He's very charming. Very...'

She pulled the curtains suddenly as if she were going to disgorge some vast secret. She held the edges closed with her hands for a moment.

'One of the troubles about falling in love and all that sort of thing is that a sort of mad mist in your head obscures ... well ... the truth. Perhaps. Of course perhaps not. I know I'm speaking out of turn.'

'I'm not eighteen Mother. I know what I'm doing.'

'I hope so.'

She let go of the curtains and came over to me. She put her hand for a moment on my head and then moved towards the door.

'We all want our children to be happy. They don't always realise that.' She opened the door. 'I suppose your father and I have been very lucky.'

Certainly they are content with themselves and with each other. They read the newspapers and watch the news on television, but their absorption in themselves and in the country of the past protects them from the reality of this world. They have, of course, in the last ten years or so attended a lot of funerals, each one opening doors onto that country that was their past, each one diminishing the circle of their friends and family; after each one they seem themselves diminished, but only physically.

They have had no direct experience of cruelty, of the violence that puzzles them so much when they hear about it second hand. Nowadays they smile with a certain melancholy, but they do still smile. Molly guards them with the ferocity of a dragon.

'Don't tell them,' she will say when there has been a crisis with a grandchild or a robbery with violence three or four streets away. 'Don't worry them. They'll only be upset.'

I admire and almost envy their equilibrium.

I have often wondered if my father had spoken his mind about Martyn would I have listened to him.

I don't suppose so.

He always left that sort of conversation to my mother, hiding from us behind veils of courtesy, smoke, newspapers and the pages of detective stories. When we were children he escaped from us to the office, to the club, fishing or golf. When he did spend time with us he was always calm, friendly and very well mannered.

*　　　*　　　*

A tinkling piano in the next apartment...
　Those stumbling words that told you what my heart meant ...
　A song saunters into my head.
　A serenade for strings...

34

My feet itch to dance.
Such foolish things.
Robin sits up straight and rattles the ice in her glass.
Such tinkling ice cubes remind me of...
'You've been asleep,' she says.
'No, no, no.'
She takes a long, tinkling drink.
'I was just wandering in the past.'
A waiter whistling as the last bar closes.
I hold up my glass towards her.
'Welcome home, darling.'
She doesn't say anything, just takes another drink. Her face now has a little colour in it.
'Tell me about the funeral.'
'There's not much you can say about a funeral really.'
'A very English attitude.'
'I am English.'
'I suppose you are.'
'What do you want to know? Your flowers arrived. Thanks. And Granny's.'
The scent of lilac and decaying roses.
She stands up suddenly and puts her glass on the mantelpiece. She walks to the centre of the room and then turns and comes back to the fireplace. 'I can't sit any longer, I feel unsettled, impatient.'
'Were there many people there?'
She doesn't answer. She takes another few steps across the room and back again.

35

'A good crowd? I'd like to think there was a good crowd.'

It is starting to get dark.

I stretch out my hand and switch on the lamp on the table.

'A good crowd,' she whispers.

I realise that she is crying.

I put down my glass and stand up.

We stand there side by side in front of the fire and the light from the lamp makes a golden pool on the floor by our feet.

A waiter whistling as the last bar closes.

I put my arm around her shoulder.

'Darling.'

Why do we find it so hard to say the things that need to be said?

I fumble in my pocket for a handkerchief.

'Here.'

She pushes it away, pushes me away.

'Star, for heaven's sake leave me alone. I have a handkerchief of my own, if I need one. I'm just shagged. It's been a bloody awful few days. Nightmares, sleeping and waking. You couldn't understand. I mean...'

She wipes the tears from her cheeks with her fingers.

'Yes, there were lots of people at the funeral. My hand is sore from being shaken. No, we didn't have an Irish party afterwards. I came here. Everyone else went home. Duty done. What else do you want to know?'

She sits down again abruptly and rubs at her eyes.

'You'll make your eyes sore...'

'My eyes are sore. My head is sore.'

I hand her the glass from the mantelpiece.

'Thanks. You killed him, you know.'

I open my mouth to speak, but she holds up her hand.

'You bloody Irish. Blew him to bits and those pathetic birds. Who gives a shit about a bird or two? Sitting at traffic lights minding his own business.'

'Listen...'

'No. That's all we ever do. Listen to you lot yapping about rights and wrongs. Listen to the gunshots and the sound of bombs going off and innocent people screaming in pain. I don't know why I'm here. I felt I was betraying him as I walked down the ramp to the plane. Then I thought if I don't go now, I'll never go, so I forced my feet to go on walking. You made him so unhappy and now this...'

She really is crying now, tears bursting out of her eyes and great hiccuping sobs. I take the glass from her hand and shove the handkerchief back into it. I stoop down and kiss her hair, then smooth it with my trembling fingers.

'We have to help each other.' I whisper the words. 'Darling, we mustn't fight.'

'I don't want to fight. He never wanted to

37

fight. I just want to tell you what I think of you. That's why I came. I think you are the only person in the world I really hate.'

I take my hand from her head.

I think of the feathers drifting through my life. White, soft feathers curling on the air.

These foolish things remind me . . .

'I'm going to make a cup of tea,' I say.

*   *   *

'A big smile, please.'

Outside the town hall in Kensington.

Winter sunshine and a little east wind blowing dust along the pavement.

I had a wide gold wedding ring on my finger and a bunch of red roses. They had no smell. I would rather have had sweetly smelling stephanotis or freesia, but Martyn had insisted on roses.

He had a bud, just bursting open, in his buttonhole.

In the picture I have, somewhere in the bottom of a drawer, he is smiling directly at the camera and I am looking a little anxiously at him.

Anxious to please. I am sure no other anxiety was in my head.

I was cold.

The east wind made me shiver suddenly and he put his arm around me. I remember feeling

38

the warmth of his hand through my silk jacket as he clasped my arm.

'Mrs Glover.'

He turned me away from the cameraman towards Angela and his partner George who were standing behind us.

'Mrs Glover,' he repeated.

The car drew up to the kerb and he opened the door for me to get in.

Quickly I shook hands with George and then I handed my flowers to Angela.

'No point in throwing them at you. Thank you so much for all the organising you've done for us. We'd never have managed without you.'

Her eyes were full of tears.

Daft, I thought, how people cry at weddings. I leant forward and kissed her.

I got into the car. Martyn patted her shoulder.

He said nothing.

'Have a great time,' said George.

Martyn got into the car and slammed the door.

We waved.

They waved.

We were on our way to Jamaica for our honeymoon.

An airline ticket to romantic places.

*　　　*　　　*

39

Even if she doesn't need a cup of tea, I do.

I hear her sobs across the hall.

Such violence tears at the veils, cracks the carefully constructed walls, makes us use words like hate, makes us see glimpses of the ugliness we carry round inside us.

I run the water into the hollow kettle.

I will make a big pot. I want to fill up the hollow inside myself with boiling liquid.

I press the switch and a little red eye glares at me.

If she weren't here, crouching in my sitting-room, I would dance now.

I would dance the death of love and trust, dance humiliation, dance white feathers floating from the sky, lying on the dark wind, dance ashes as they fly and then settle on the wounded tarmac of a London street.

That's what I would wish to dance, but hard as I might try, my body settles for the mundane quick, slow shuffle of 'It's Only a Paper Moon.'

Anyway the kettle whistle prevents any flights of fancy . . .

I warm the teapot, my hands comforted by the warmth of the red china as I rock the pot in my hands.

'I'm sorry, Star.'

She is standing in the doorway.

I empty the hot water into the sink and reach for the tea caddy.

'That's all right.'

Three spoons of tea. One for each person and one for the pot.

'I haven't cried till now.'

I pour boiling water into the pot, scented steam rises.

'You don't have to say anything.'

'I never cry. He taught me not to cry.'

I get two mugs from the cupboard and put them on the table.

'Yes. He would have done that. Tears embarrassed him.'

'I didn't mean any of that rubbish.'

'It's all right, darling, really it is.'

'It was all rubbish. I got carried away...'

'Have a cup of tea. I do understand. There are times...'

'Star...'

'I wish you wouldn't call me Star.'

'He...'

'Yes. I know what he did, he said. I just don't like to be called that name. Tea? Did I offer you tea?'

'No tea.'

'Sometimes, it's a comfort.'

She doesn't answer.

I pour myself a mugful, then a tincture of milk.

'Another drink?'

She shakes her head.

'Let's go back and sit down.'

I almost have to push past her and I hear her

footsteps shuffling after me as I cross the hall. I sit down by the fire and she begins to pace, her hands loosely clasped in front of her, ten steps along the room past the windows now, becoming dusky, past my desk and the ordered piles of paper, turn; ten paces back to the door. I sip the tea and watch her, watch the whirl of her skirt as she turns, watch her fingers now loose, now clenched together. I think of the tiger in the zoo I used to visit as a child, pacing backwards and forwards in his cage, his tail from time to time lashing as he walked and turned, walked and turned in an energy of despair. I watch her through the steam from my mug of tea. The room is becoming a prison, for me as well as for her.

'What do you say to a quick dash down the pier before it gets totally dark? Clear your head. Help you to sleep. Blow...'

'Yes. Nothing, no wind will blow away the stuff in my head, but yes, I'd like to walk. Or maybe even run. You'll have to lend me a pair of shoes.'

*   *   *

The pier, for those unfamiliar with it, curves out into the bay a mile or so, protecting one side of the harbour, which holds, in the summer months, hundreds of neatly moored yachts that make their music as they rock

42

drowsily with the movement of the sea. The ungainly car ferries crouch inshore at their terminals and move at given moments like prehistoric monsters across the harbour and through the narrow entrance ... our gateway to the world.

The pier we walk along is two-tiered, wide, solid, nothing you feel could ever damage it or the squat lighthouse at the harbour entrance.

To the lighthouse and back ... no excuses, except when mad high seas crash over the protecting granite blocks on the seaward side and the high wall and flood the pier itself with foaming water. Then I stay at home.

To the lighthouse and back.

Some words lurk in the darkness of your mind, like young men lurk in the shadows, waiting to damage, maim, or merely frighten unsuspecting walkers once the light has gone.

Words can be like missiles or roses or travellers to another world. You can play delightful games with them, that will make you and others smile, feel light-hearted, or you can kill; you can hide the truth or manifest it. Describing the landscape is safe, I think; such words cannot be misconstrued. So I think about this landscape, the lamp-posts, just sprung into evening life and the bandstands and the huge blocks of granite that on a summer day sparkle in the light.

She walks beside me and we don't speak

dangerous words to each other. Her head is slightly bent forward so that she cannot catch sight either of the landscape or of me.

Twenty minutes to the lighthouse and twenty minutes back.

Better than pacing round my room.

Space here really to stretch the legs.

Her eyes are still raw from crying.

Rather than think any more about words and landscape, I decide to speak.

'I never realised how much I missed the pier until the first time I walked it after I came back here. Alone. I was alone and quite ... well ... unsure ... of myself. I was wondering if after all those years away, would I be able to live here. Would I be forgiven by these stones for going away.'

I laugh aloud at myself. Why would the stones care, I hear her saying silently in her head.

A light flashes from the lighthouse, the first this evening, and then another ...

'Then I felt the familiarity creeping through my feet as I walked. It was going to be all right. I have walked this pier for ever. I will walk it for ever.'

Another flash.

'What rubbish you talk.'

'I suppose so. I won't say another word.'

We reach the lighthouse in silence and stand for a moment looking at the sea, the curling

44

waves and the city lights rimming the bay and then we turn and walk back in silence.

Twenty minutes there. Twenty minutes back.

*   *   *

'I think I should meet your family, Martyn. It seems so odd to have been married to you for six months and never...'

'Is it six months? Six weeks is what it seems like. Let's go out and celebrate.'

Our flat was in a mansion block looking down towards Camden Town. In the daylight trains moved below us, slowly manoeuvring across the complexities of plaited tracks.

He hadn't liked the notion of living underground as he called it, so we had moved into his flat when we returned from Jamaica.

'I have no family. You know that, Star. You are my family. I have no one else.'

'Uncles? Aunts? Even a distant cousin? There must...'

He came over and put his arms around me. He nuzzled his face into my neck.

'Only you. You are all I have.'

He sang the words softly and I felt his warm breath on my neck and shoulder. I felt his words glowing on my skin.

'*Only you, beneath the moon and under the sun.*'

45

I used to love to watch the trains, the signals moving up and down, the points shifting the engines from track to track...

I used to sit and watch in the evenings when I got home from work before him. I would pretend not to hear him coming in, pretend not to hear him as he came across the floor towards me and then I would scream with fright when he put his arms around me and held me tight.

He seemed to enjoy such pretences.

He never wanted to know what I did at the office, nor did he ever tell me anything that went on in his office.

'I buy things. I sell things. That's all you need to know,' he said once. 'That's all anyone does in this world, they buy things or they sell things. I do both.'

'I don't do either of those things.'

He laughed.

'Of course you do, Star. You buy the services of writers for as little as you can and you try to sell their books for as much as you can. The publisher who doesn't succeed in doing that will go to the wall. There's no room for gentlemen, no room for propriety any longer in the world. Don't fool yourself that there is.'

He took my hand and kissed it.

'Make what you can, while you can. That's the way of it. Then indulge in your dreams, your fantasies, if you have any. Get the hard stuff first. Enough to last you, enough to indulge yourself. That's what I'm at. One day you'll see.'

'See what?'

'I will be one of the great illusionists of the world. Wait and see. People trampling over each other to see me. Name in lights.'

As he spoke the last words he held his hand out in front of me. A long-stemmed red rose grew between his fingers.

*   *   *

My mother used to write regularly to me; about once a month her letter would arrive. Terse notes they were, rather than letters to be savoured and reread.

Dear Stella, your father has a nasty cold which has kept him home from the office all week. In spite of this we went to the Abbey on Thursday to see the new play by Frank Carney, that everyone is scandalised by. The name escapes me. I can't say that I thought very much of it. Francine is pregnant again. We are all thrilled and hope that this time it will be a girl. Nolan comes next week to paint the hall and landings. I hope your father's cold will be better by then, as the smell of paint gives him headaches if he is around the house all day. Do write, dear, if you have time.

47

That sort of thing...

I seldom wrote to her.

Everything to do with home seemed so far away and inconsequential.

I really admired Martyn's surgical detachment from his family and background. He had a courage I believed that I could never acquire, to wield the scalpel, excise from his life the weighty baggage of the past.

Clever, I thought at that time; a trick worth knowing.

*　　*　　*

The gate always squeals when you push it open and then squeals again when you close it behind you to keep out stray dogs.

'You should oil that.'

They are the first words she has spoken for half an hour.

'I have. I do frequently. It makes no difference.'

'It's a ghastly noise.'

'A sort of natural burglar alarm.'

We walk up the two shallow steps to my hall door and I turn the key in the lock.

I am so lucky to have the ground floor of this old, handsome house and my own yard, my own tree and my own squealing gate.

I suppose I could have the gate rehung, renew the ancient hinges.

Such domestic imperfections don't bother me...

They used to bother Martyn.

The dripping tap.

The drawer that sticks.

The grey streaking above a radiator.

A broken sash cord.

Such foolish things.

'I think I'll stay until tomorrow.'

Her words surprise me.

'Darling, I never thought you'd be going back tonight.'

'That was my plan. My original...'

She throws her coat onto the bentwood coatstand and stoops to take off my shoes.

'Stay for ages,' I say rashly.

'I have to get back to work.'

She walks in her stocking feet into the sitting-room.

'I really only meant to stay a couple of hours. Just to ... just to...'

She sits down by the fire and rubs her sore eyes with the back of her hand.

'... to say hello. Yes. To say hello, but I don't think I could face that trek tonight.'

'Why don't you go and have a nice big bath and I'll bring you your supper in bed.'

She looks up at me with a faint smile.

'Motherspeak.'

'We have our uses.'

'Why do people have to die?'

'The world would be a little overcrowded if they didn't.'

49

'No. I mean before their time ... untimely. I know it's an unanswerable question, but my mind just keeps asking it. Why? Why? I'm going to miss him so much.'

'Yes. I suppose you will. But ...'

'That act of his with the birds was fabulous, wasn't it?'

'Yes.'

'Do you want to know how ...?'

'No.'

She gets up.

'I think I'll go and have that bath.'

*   *   *

He had this room at the back of the flat, facing north. I was never in it. It must have been quite dark, with steely northern light pressing through the two windows. I always presumed there must have been two windows as I think the room must have been the mirror image of our sitting-room, and it had two windows facing more cheerfully south over the railway tracks and the domes and spires of London. And over to the right the trees of Primrose Hill.

He kept the door of that room locked; something that upset me at first, but I came to accept it, to forget the prickle of hurt I had felt when he first told me.

'I have to have somewhere private, where I can work undisturbed.'

'I won't disturb you. You should know that.'

50

'I'm sure you wouldn't, darling, but I prefer to keep it locked. I don't want anyone poking and prying.'

I felt tears coming up behind my eyes.

'I wouldn't poke or pry either. If you tell me not to go into the room, I assure you I won't do it. Believe me.'

'Of course I believe you.'

He turned the key in the lock just the same and dropped it into his pocket.

'I have to have my own privacy you know. I need to have my own space.' He smiled at me. 'You must believe me.'

'I do, but...'

'But what, my darling?'

'Nothing. It's OK.'

When I look back at the past I wonder, linger on moments, say to myself, if at that moment I had said what passed through my head, if I had played the game another way, would it have changed the pattern? At that moment, I remember, I had felt a breath of guilt for having forced him to use words like privacy, space, for in some way not being quite the loving, understanding person that he had taken me for.

He used to spend a lot of time in that room, mostly to begin with on his own, but there were two men who used to arrive, nod to me in the hall and disappear into the room and then, if I were around, they would nod at me again as they left the flat a couple of hours later.

Dr Rhodes, one of them was called, and Peter Magill.

They didn't cause me any bother. I never had to make cups of tea for them or pour drinks. They just passed across the hall nodding. Sometimes they carried boxes, suitcases or long rolls of paper. I used to imagine them creating illusions behind that door; one day making Dr Rhodes disappear or wrapping Peter Magill in sheets of paper and throwing him out of the window. In my head I saw bears, bats, cats, monkeys, screens of smoke and sly spotlights, but in reality all I heard was the occasional low murmur of their voices and sometimes Martyn's laughter.

He was always in good spirits after these sessions.

*   *   *

I am a good cook, a caring cook.

I treat the ingredients with respect. I clean them well; I slice, peel, chop with attention and panache.

I make soups and pâtés and pies.

My kitchen smells slightly of garlic and Italian olive oil; small pots of herbs stand on my windowsill; I have three sharp knives of varying sizes, a huge jug full of wooden spoons and a garlic crusher that someone gave me once, but I never use.

I taught myself to cook when we moved to

the country and I had time on my hands; nothing to do but look after the child and worry about his bloody birds.

Now, I have soup to comfort her and thick fillet steaks rubbed with garlic and crushed pink peppercorns.

I usually listen to music while I cook, fairly fortissimo, as I prefer music to be foreground rather than background.

Elly Ameling singing Schubert, Mozart's Great Mass or the sound of Callas fill the flat and my head at times to such an extent that I have to stop chopping or stirring and stand quite still in the middle of the room listening with my entire body.

This evening though I work in silence, listening with anxiety for any sounds of distress from Robin and not quite knowing what I will do if I hear anything that disturbs me. But I only hear the splash of water as she moves in the bath.

It's strange I have never, since her childhood, seen her in a bath, never walked unthinkingly into a bathroom and surprised her wet and gleaming, her hair tied in a bundle on the top of her head. I have never had that moment of recollection or recognition of my own younger body.

I make French dressing, mashing the garlic in a heavy white bowl and she splashes in the bath a few yards away. She is full of sorrow and anger and I am, at this moment, at the mercy of weary memories.

* * *

He came into the bathroom as I was washing my feet, gently pushing the flannel between my toes. I have never liked washing my feet; never much liked my feet, useful but undecorative, bony and lumpy, potentially problematic, potentially painful.

The room was quite small and steam covered the window and the mirrors. He appeared through the mist still wearing his dressing-gown.

'How can you bear that heat?'

He sat down by the bath and trailed his hands in the water.

'I love it. Gets rid of all impurities.'

'You look cooked.'

He touched my shoulder and then ran his fingers up my neck and into my hair. He pulled at the ribbon that held my hair on top of my head.

'Hey. Don't do that.'

I jerked my head away from him.

He pulled again and the knot opened and my hair fell down around my neck and shoulders.

'I'm trying to keep it dry.'

I stood up and reached for my towel.

He pulled it from my hand and tried to push me down again into the water.

'You look wonderful. All shining, like

mother of pearl.'

'Please give me my towel. I'm going to be late for work.'

'What does work matter? Get your priorities right.'

'I have my priorities right.'

'No. No. No.'

There was a real anger in his voice that startled me, but I grabbed the towel from him and wrapped it round myself. At that moment I didn't feel like standing naked beside him. I didn't want his eyes and hands touring my body.

He put out a hand towards me, but I slipped past him and went into the bedroom.

He stood in silence in the doorway watching me dress.

'You've never said no to me before,' he said eventually.

'There's a first time for everything.'

I was throwing things into my bag; comb, Kleenex, keys, purse, where the hell's my...

'I could have made you.'

No purse, lipstick, powder, chequebook.

'Star.'

'You could. It would have been a pretty silly thing to do.'

I got my coat from the wardrobe. My purse was there, flat as poverty in my pocket.

'I love you. What's silly about that?'

'I love you too, darling. Can you lend me ten bob? I'll have to take a taxi.'

'I have no money.'

'Don't be tiresome Martyn, of course you've got money. I'll give it back to you this evening.'

I went across the room to where his trousers lay over the back of a chair and I picked them up. Coins rattled in a pocket. I put my hand into the pocket and took out a handful of change. He ran across the room and snatched the trousers from my hand.

'How dare you...'

'I'm...' I laughed nervously.

'Don't ever do that. Ever, do you hear me? Don't take things out of my pocket. Don't put your spying hands into my pockets. Don't...' He threw the trousers across the room. 'Ever...'

I stood and looked at him, the coins in my hand. His face was pale, his eyes like grey stones, bulging slightly in his head. I dropped the money into my pocket and picked up my bag.

'This has got a bit absurd,' I said. 'I'll see you this evening.'

I went out of the room and across the hall. As I opened the door he called me from the room.

'Come back, Star. Please come back to me Star.'

For a moment I hesitated and then I opened the door and went out. My hand shook as I held the door knob and pulled the door shut quietly behind me.

I didn't see him for two days.

I didn't sleep for two nights, full of anxiety, full of self-recrimination.

When he did come home, he gave no explanation, no excuses. He was loving, cheerful, full of energy, secretive.

* * *

The bathroom door opens and I hear Robin crossing the hall.

Shuff, shuff across the black and white tiles. Handsome tiles, bought after a BBC adaptation of one of my books. Shuff, shuff, slippers.

'Ring Granny,' I call out to her.

She comes into the kitchen swathed in towels, her face pink and moist and very young. The slippers are my blue towelling ones.

I remember her at twelve years old, her hair sticking out around her head, her face pink and moist, her humour volatile. If he were there she would hurl herself onto his knee, or put her arms around his neck and swing her feet off the ground. He would laugh. He would discover little gold-wrapped coins, or chocolate eggs, little glittering treasures tumbling from her damp hair.

I used to smile at such charming exhibitions, though I don't suppose either of them noticed.

'I'll call her in a minute,' says Robin. 'How

are they both?'

'Well. Slow now, but well. I know they'd love to see you. I hope you'll have time...'

'Probably. I'll talk to her and we'll see. What are you making?'

'Soup, steak and a salad. I hope that's OK.'

'Divine. You can always trust old Momma to come up with the right food at the right time.'

I feel my face going red.

She touches my shoulder lightly.

'I have often wondered, down the years, who you cherished after you left us.'

'Myself. Go and ring your grandmother before they settle to their bridge. They hate to be interrupted in the middle of a game. Don't forget to send your love to Molly.'

She looks at me as if she were about to make some sarcastic remark, but she thinks better of it and goes into the sitting-room to telephone.

*   *   *

It was a fine spring evening and I had walked home from Bloomsbury, across Regent's Park and up the wide roads of St John's Wood. The magnolias were just bursting into flower; London at its best just stirring after its winter sleep. Even Chalk Farm didn't look too bad.

The flat was stuffy, full of clinging winter smells.

I went into the sitting-room and turned on

the radio, someone was playing Elgar's cello concerto. I turned it up fortissimo and opened the windows. Far below me a diesel tanker pulling three goods wagons came slowly round the bend and moved across the web of tracks. I leaned out across the windowsill and watched it.

Snake.

Snake among high dirty walls, burdened with the remains of old trees and dusty city hedges.

Snake in the music leads the old tanker into the tunnel; papers blow in the light wind, a light turns from green to red. How strong you must have to be to play a cello, to command and control such resonances. The tracks are empty now and a distant whistle blows from the marshalling yards of Euston station, or maybe Camden goods yards.

The music stopped.

Nothing then but the humming of the streets.

'What on earth are you hanging out the window like that for?'

'Looking.'

I turn back into the silence of the room.

'I couldn't hear myself think with that noise.'

'I'm sorry, I didn't know you were in.'

'Is that what you do when I'm not around, deafen yourself with music?'

'Sometimes.'

59

'What was it?'

He didn't wait for an answer.

'I'm freezing.'

As he shut the windows down a train screamed out of the tunnel, running north this time, at speed.

Holyhead? I wondered. Home.

'What time are we eating?'

'Well ... whatever time suits you.'

'You tell me. You're the cook.'

'Three quarters of an hour ... say half past seven ... or thereabouts.'

He had his hand on the doorknob of his secret room.

'Make it eight thirty. I have...' He gestured with his head towards the door.

'All right.'

'Sure?'

'Of course.'

He went into the room and shut the door behind him. I could hear the low murmur of voices.

*   *   *

I, then, danced in the bathroom, radio turned down low, so as not to disturb Dr Rhodes or Peter Magill or whoever might be there. Music might take their minds off their mysteries. The bathroom was small so it was a reduced form of dancing, swaying, arms stretching and twisting, feet merely twitching rather than stepping out, no sliding, no twirling. I partnered myself in the glass until the steam eliminated my reflection.

Such seriously foolish things remind me of you.

As I lay in the bath I thought of them doing hand exercises, limbering their fingers; fluidity, speed, now you see it and now you don't.

Mirrors, lights, springs, boxes and drawers with false bottoms remind me of you.

Maybe, of course, I thought, as I lay in the delicious scented water, they were plotting to take over the world.

Plotters.

They didn't look like plotters.

After I got out of the bath I opened the window to allow the steam to escape.

* * *

I hear her voice in the hall, quietly answering my mother's questions.

I do hope she will have time to see those old people. After all, she has no other old people in her life. Martyn's elimination of his past was total. I often wondered how he knew his name was Glover. Had he invented it? Not a name I would have invented for myself. Had I been so inclined I would have chosen a name with a little more magic attached to it, a rhythm, a hint of glory. Was it he rather than some inadequate mother who had put the Y in

Martyn? I learnt quite soon not to ask such questions.

'I have invented myself,' he once said to me. 'There is no need for you to pry into how I achieved this trick.'

*   *   *

I rang Mother one sunny evening.

The flat had been empty when I returned from work.

I listened carefully at the secret door, but I could hear no sounds from the room.

The sun gilded my fingers as I dialled the number. I liked that; Benvenuto Cellini made this hand, so I was laughing when my mother answered the telephone.

'Hello?'

'Mother.'

'Stella. How odd you sound. It's not the cheap time. Are you all right?'

'I'm fine. Great in fact. It's a beautiful evening.'

'I presume you haven't rung me to tell me about the weather in London.'

She hated people spending their money foolishly.

'If you'd waited ten minutes it would have been the cheap time.'

'Yes. So it would. Are you well, darling?'

'Perfectly well, thank you.'

'And Daddy?'

62

'Well, well, well.' Her voice was impatient. 'Daddy's been made captain.'

'Captain of what?'

'The golf club, of course.'

'Congratulate him from me.'

'Well?'

'Well what?'

'Have you something to say? You must have something to say.'

'Yes. Bill took me...'

'Bill, dear? You must be clear.'

'Senior partner. Top cat. The boss of bosses ... Anyway ... Lunch ... We had lunch and he asked me if I'd like to be a partner.'

'Yes,' she said and then after a moment. 'That's good, dear. That sounds very good. You should be very pleased.'

'Thrilled. Imagine. He said such nice things about me. I'm still in a whirl and a bit drunk ... with astonishment as well as wine. I'm all dizzy in my head.'

'It's wonderful news. I'm so pleased for you. Daddy will be thrilled and proud. I'm proud too. Have you told um ... er ...'

I felt a small stir of anger.

'Martyn,' she said, just in the nick of time.

'Not yet. He wasn't in the office when I rang him. His secretary said he'd ring me back but he hasn't. I had to tell someone. That's why I couldn't even wait that ten minutes...'

'Have you decided? That's important too.'

'Yes. Yes of course. Not officially. I don't

have to say officially until the end of the week. I'm supposed to be thinking seriously, but yes.'

'We'll see.'

'What does that mean?'

'It means we'll see at the end of the week. Ring me on Sunday, dear. It's cheap all day on Sunday. I'll tell your father when he comes in and then you can speak to him on Sunday. We will be waiting to hear.' There was a pause and I thought she might have rung off. Then she said, 'Be sensible. You're not always very sensible. This is costing. Love, dear child. Don't forget.'

She put down the receiver.

I stood looking at the receiver in my golden fingers for a moment.

'You're not always sensible either.' I hung up.

About an hour later the telephone rang.

The sun had now shifted, soon I would have to turn on the lights.

It was Angela.

'Hello, is that, ah, Mrs Glover?'

'Yes, hello Angela.'

'How clever of you to recognise my voice.'

'One of my minor talents.'

She didn't laugh.

'He asked me to ring you ... oh ages ago. I must apologise, I've been up to my eyes and I...'

'He?' I sounded like my mother. 'Who is he?'

'Mr ... Martyn, of course. I'm really terribly

sorry. I hope you haven't got the dinner ready or anything...' She paused and I waited unhelpfully in the silence.

'A client rang and he had to rush out to meet him. He won't be back for...'

'Did you give him my message?'

There was silence.

'I rang just after lunch, if you remember, and asked you to ask him to ring me. Did you do that? It was important.'

'Of course I did.'

'You weren't too busy?'

'I gave him your message. I always give...'

'Unless you're too busy.'

She thought about this for a moment.

'Are you attacking me in some way?'

'I'm just trying to find out if you gave Martyn my message.'

'I have told you twice that I did. If Martyn didn't ring you, he's the one you should be blaming, not me.'

'Yes. Well, thanks,' I said and put down the receiver.

When he arrived home several hours later, he was angry. Eyes like flint, his face red with either anger or alcohol.

I was in bed reading.

I could see his flinty eyes from where I lay.

I put my book down.

'Had a good evening?'

He didn't answer.

He took off his jacket and hung it carefully

65

over the back of a chair.

'Darling?'

'You were rude to Angela.'

He began to wrestle with his tie. He had definitely had a certain amount to drink.

'Not very.'

'She was doing her job and you were rude to her. She was very upset.'

He threw his tie onto the floor.

'She wasn't doing her job very well. I was upset too. I rang you at lunch-time. Did she give you my message? That was all I asked her.'

'Yes, she did.'

He pulled the money from his trousers pocket and jangled it onto the dressing-table.

'Then why didn't you ring me back?'

'I was busy. I work. I don't just sit around all day reading bloody manuscripts. I work. I make money. A lot of money. Sometimes I don't have time to spare for chatting.'

He sat down and began to unlace his shoes.

'I don't normally ring you just to chat.'

'She said you slammed down the phone.'

'Oh, for heaven's sake...'

He threw one shoe across the room and then the other.

'She rang me at seven thirty to say you wouldn't be back for dinner.'

'So?'

He pulled off his trousers and his socks and left them in a heap on the floor. As he walked towards the bed he was unbuttoning his shirt.

'What do you mean, so?'

'I mean what's all the fuss about? What's the big deal? I mean what right have you to tick off my secretary?'

He dropped his shirt on the floor and got into bed.

'In case you don't know the answer to that, it's none. No right. Remember that in future.'

He turned on his side away from me, pulling the bedclothes tight up round his neck.

'Turn off the light,' he said. 'I can never get to sleep with the light on.'

*   *   *

Robin comes into the kitchen.

'Granny sounds well. I said I'd go and have lunch with them tomorrow.'

'Good. They will be so pleased. They will submit you to serious interrogation. You'd better be prepared to unveil all your secrets.'

She picks a leaf of lettuce from the bowl and dips it in dressing and puts it in her mouth.

'Mmmm.'

Dressing dribbles down her chin. She catches it with a finger and licks it.

'You do make marvellous dressing.'

'If you eat it all now, there won't be any left for dinner.'

'More motherspeak.'

'I happen to be your mother.'

She takes another lettuce leaf.

67

'It's the garlic. I do love garlic.'

She dips again and crunches again and again. The dressing dribbles over her chin.

'I hope I don't live to be as ancient as the grandparents.'

'I expect you'll change your mind on that with the passing of the years.'

'You could have taught me to cook, to make dressing like that, if you hadn't run away like that.'

'What fun that would have been.'

'Think how different I might be now.'

'Think how different I might be now.'

*   *   *

'My beautiful Star.'

Those were the words he spoke the next morning.

The words woke me and then he pulled me tight against his body.

I could see the blue sky outside the window and a whistle wailed as the 7.45 to somewhere pulled out of the tunnel. I usually heard it as I filled the kettle for my breakfast cup of tea.

'Star,' he breathed into my ear.

I should have been up, but I was lost in his breath and his hands. The sky was streaked with crimson.

Red sky in the morning...

The trains came and went below us, their delectable sounds rising, our sounds and cries

68

mingling and wailing.

I was late for work.

Red sky in the morning.

I had to take another taxi.

*   *   *

He was home before me that evening, sitting in my chair by the window.

Surprisingly the window was open and he sat, relaxed in the chair, almost as if he were enjoying the evening air. I threw my coat onto a chair and he got up and came towards me, his empty hands outstretched. Without a word he took my hands in his and stooping kissed them, each finger in turn, nails, knuckles, then turned them over and kissed the palms, his lips burrowing amongst the lines of future and past. He held my hands clasped tight in his and looked up smiling into my face. As I smiled back at his I felt my hands filling with cold stones and I looked down and blue and green glittered and overflowed like cold water splashing through my fingers.

'Stars,' he said.

It was a beautiful string of beads, aquamarine, jade, opal, and turquoise.

'Darling.'

'And tears. My tears. Never leave me, Star.'

'Oh, darling...'

He took my arm and led me to the chair in which he had been sitting. He pushed me down

69

into it and then closed down the window. The stones were warming in my hands.

'Now,' he said, 'for something new.'

He pointed across the room towards the hall and across the dark hall towards the door of his room.

As I looked the door opened and a man appeared.

Was it Dr Rhodes or Peter Magill? I leaned forward to get a better look, but the face was veiled in what seemed to be mist.

Behind me I could hear Martyn making a soft whistling sound between his teeth. Just for a moment I heard it. The man in the doorway held his hands out towards me and I saw that a small fire burned in the palm of each hand. Martyn was silent now.

All of a sudden a bird burst from each of the burning hands, white, they soared through the mist towards the ceiling and then swooped towards me.

I dropped the string of beads clattering onto the floor and covered my face with my hands.

'No. Oh, no.'

I felt the breath of their wings as they passed my head and then I heard a murmur of pleasure from Martyn.

Cautiously I uncovered my face and looked round at him.

One of the white birds perched on his wrist, the other clawed quite impatiently at his sleeve.

'I'm sorry. I hate birds. They frighten me

almost to death.'

'They won't do you any harm. You mustn't be upset by birds. Beautiful creatures. Aren't you, so sooo beautiful. My sweet doves.'

He walked slowly past me towards the hall. I saw that the door of his room was closed. No man, no mist, no flames, just Martyn gently carrying his doves across the hall.

At the door he turned.

'I'll be with you in a tick,' he said.

He opened the door and went in, closing it carefully behind him. I could hear the sound of voices, a little laugh.

I picked the beads up from the floor and waited to see what would happen next.

After a while the door opened again and Dr Rhodes came out. He was wearing a long mackintosh and carried a cardboard box under his arm. Without looking in my direction he walked across the dark space and disappeared out through the hall door. He made no sound.

Was he also an illusion, I wondered, a fragment of glass, a sliver of reflected light. I heard the lift humming on its way up to collect him. That made me smile.

Martyn came out of the room. He locked the door behind him and dropped the key into his pocket.

'Well?' he called over to me.

He switched on all the lights as he moved towards me. His face was glowing with excitement.

71

'Brilliant. Wonderful.'

'You really mean it?'

'Oh, yes of course, darling. It was amazing. Like magic. How did you do it?'

He rumpled his fingers through my hair.

'Ask me no questions and I'll tell you no lies.'

I had never seen him look so pleased.

He wasn't so pleased later on that evening when I got round to telling him my news. We had finished eating and I had pushed the dirty dishes to the end of the table. I sat beside him and put my hand on his. His hands were soft like a woman's, with long, bony fingers and neat, shining nails. His hand trembled as I touched it.

For a long time after I had spoken he was silent. He pulled his hand away from mine and seemed to stare down at his splayed fingers, looking for a message to grow there. Nothing would have surprised me. I touched his finger to remind him of my presence and he moved his hand slightly out of my reach. Our hands lay side by side on the flowered cloth and there were no messages.

'Well. That's great. A partner. Great.'

He lifted his head as he spoke and looked at me. The blue had left his eyes, but maybe that was just a trick of light. He gave my hand a little pat and got up from the table.

'Yes. Terrific. I honestly think that's terrific. I always knew you were destined for great

72

things.'

'Seriously, Martyn...'

'I am serious. Of course. We must celebrate.'

He went into the kitchen and I heard him opening cupboards.

'I haven't made up my mind yet,' I called after him. 'I'm still mulling it over.'

He came back with a bottle of red wine, two glasses and a corkscrew. He began the business of uncorking the bottle.

'Of course you must say yes, if you want to.'

The cork came out and he filled the glasses, each almost to its brim.

'I have till Monday.'

'Monday.'

He pushed a glass towards me.

My hands were trembling and I spilled some of the wine on the tablecloth as I lifted the glass to my lips.

'Clumsy Star.' He smiled and raised his glass towards me. 'Cheers.'

'Cheers.' The wine ran over my fingers.

'What will this ... um ... elevation mean? Forgive me, darling, for asking such a silly question. I know nothing, as you...'

'Well, I'll be involved in decision making, the house policy, that sort of thing. Each house has its own strong identity and integrity. I'll ...'

He was sprinkling salt on the wine stain on the cloth.

'... I'll be more involved with the writers,

have responsibility for...'

He patted the salt down onto the cloth with a fingertip. The pink started to seep up through the tiny crystals.

'... new writers ... power, I suppose, I'll have a bit of power. I'll have my own room, my own authors ... a secretary.'

He laughed.

'A secretary. How about that.'

'Yes. Soon your secretary will be able to talk to my secretary. That'll save a lot of trouble.'

He picked up his glass and held it out towards me again.

'Cheers.'

*   *   *

'We're almost ready.'

Glowing bubbles burst around the steaks in the pan.

'Why don't you hop into bed and I'll ...?'

'Here. I'll eat in here. Then I'll go to bed.'

I turned the flame low under the pan and begin to lay the table.

'To sleep perchance to dream.' She mutters the words. She is staring at me, her eyes faintly hostile. That's what they look like to me, maybe they're not, maybe they're just tired eyes.

'Candles,' I say.

I get two red candles in glass candlesticks

and put them on the table. She pours herself a glass of wine and continues to stare at me.

'Emm ... Matches.'

She takes a box of matches from the pocket of her dressing-gown and throws them to me.

Of course I miss them and they land on the table. 'Thanks.'

I light the candles and turn off most of the lights in the room.

'Let's be kind to ourselves. Sit down, darling. Relax. Actually you look much more relaxed than you did before your bath. It's amazing how ...'

'Do shut up, Star.'

'Stella.'

'Mother.'

We eat our soup in silence.

Her face flickers golden and black and her eyes are reflected flames.

'I suppose in the end of all I have a lot to thank your father for.'

She puts down her spoon and waits for me to go on.

'It occurs to me sometimes that if I had continued to work in publishing, you know, worked out my energies in that way, I might never have had to think, to realise such a possibility about myself. I might have been too absorbed in other people's creativity to find my own.'

'I always think that speculation on what might have been is a waste of time.'

75

'It's an occupation we all indulge in though, in spite of that.'

I get up and take the soup bowls from the table.

'I really enjoy being alive.'

I scoop a steak from the pan onto her plate and bring it over to her.

'I've noticed.'

'So should you. You have such attributes.'

I put my plate on the table and sit down.

'Vegetables, brown bread, salad.' I make a gesture with my hand.

'For heaven's sake, I've just come from my father's funeral and you're exhorting me to be happy.'

'Not quite. I didn't mean it to sound like that. Enjoy life. It's a different thing really. I'm not talking about today, this minute. I mean in general. Yes, in general. It's quite important to enjoy life.'

'Martyn...' She stops.

She picks up her knife and fork.

I wait but she says nothing. It was as if she had thrown me a ball and I had not put out my hand to catch it.

'Your father enjoyed his life.'

'So?'

'Lives, I should say. I always got the feeling about Martyn that he hadn't just invented one life for himself. He had several totally different lives. He was a juggler, each life had its own arc, its own passage and they never touched.'

76

'How absurd you are.'

'I was the ball that crashed to the floor. I blipped. A purely temporary blip though.'

'How can you say a thing like that?'

Because it's true, I think, but don't say to her.

'He pined for you. He mourned you. He became almost like a child. I had to mind him. I know. I was only thirteen. Remember.'

'I remember.'

'I could hardly bear to go back to school at the end of each holidays because he was so lonely. I begged him to let me stay at home. I would have gone to day school, but he wouldn't let me. I must think of my future. Your great future my darling, he used to say. We both look to your future. I was all he had.'

'Hum.'

'What do you mean, hum?'

'Nothing really. Eat your steak before it gets cold.'

'I'm not hungry any more.'

'Eat your bloody steak, Robin, and stop being such an ass. It's a terrible thing that has happened. Shocking. The memories boil, that is always painful and a violent and untimely death makes everything more painful, but don't you go trying to make me feel something ... some guilt or remorse because it isn't there for me to feel. Eat. I won't say hum any more.'

She puts her knife and fork down beside her plate and clasps her hands together.

77

'Oh God, all the clichés about children and food. If you want to punish your mother, don't eat her food. Do you remember the last big row we all had? Do you?'

She shakes her head.

I don't believe her.

'Well, it was about food. It was about punishment. It was about power. You won. Don't let's have a row tonight. Eat. It will do you good. Drink. It will do you no harm. Let's get this evening behind us.'

'He always said you understood nothing.'

'He was probably right.'

She begins to eat.

*　　*　　*

On Friday evening I loitered home through Regent's Park. The air was pink with evening sun. Lights were beginning to pop on all over the place. The first daffodils were lightening the darkness under the trees. Some young men were playing football, shouting, laughing, leaping with exuberance, their neatly folded jackets acting as goalposts. In the zoo a lion roared, a tired despairing sound.

My mother had never taken me to the zoo.

'Just think about it,' she said to me one day as I whinged at her. 'Just think about being in prison and having all those people coming to stare at you and not being able to get away from them and wanting to eat them . . .'

She had roared the last two words at me and I had jumped, startled by her rage.

Outside the door of our flats Martyn was standing by the car. He was looking moodily down the road towards the Underground station, his fingers dancing impatiently on the roof of the car.

I quickened my steps.

'Hey, hey, hey,' I called out in his direction.

He turned round and saw me running towards him. For a moment he was unable to smile.

'You're late.'

Then a big smile came and irradiated his face.

'I walked through the park. It was such a lovely evening. Anyway what's late or early?'

'I'm taking you away for the weekend.'

'Oooh! Where to?'

'Surprise. Run up and get your things, there's a good girl and let's get off. I said we'd be there in time for dinner.'

'Where to, Martyn? What things? How do I know what to bring?'

'Toothbrush. That sort of thing.'

'Ball gown? Bathing togs? Riding breeches?'

'You don't have any riding breeches ... oh ha ha. Get a move on.'

He went round to the other side of the car and got in, slamming the door. He picked up the *Evening Standard* and began to read it.

Just to tease him I put my face close to the

window of the car and said, 'Passport?'

He pretended not to hear. When I came out of the door barely ten minutes later he put the paper down, leant forward and started the engine before I was even across the pavement.

'You are in a hurry.'

I threw my bag into the back of the car and got in beside him.

'No point in dilly dallying.'

'If you had let me know, I would have rushed home. Might even have got the afternoon off.'

'Then it wouldn't have been a secret.'

'True.'

He wasn't a chatty driver. In fact he liked to drive in silence.

That suited me. I liked to look at lives and landscapes slipping past. I liked sometimes to sing inside my head.

We headed east, our backs to the setting sun, what was left of it.

Green, amber, red. We stopped and started. Beacons flashed, men and women pushed their bones home to their other lives.

I knew nothing about Hore Belisha except that he invented flashing beacons. I wondered whether to ask Martyn about him, but decided against it.

Towards the east we stopped and started.

Evening dust rose from under the wheels and feet and thickened the air.

That bright star hung in the sky.

Perhaps we were going to Bethlehem...

No. Nothing like that.

I don't much enjoy being driven into the thickening evening, not knowing if I should have my bathing togs or a ball gown. I don't much enjoy surprises. I want to be loved. I want to keep the air around me clear. I am a dull sod.

I thought those morose sort of thoughts for a while as we red, amber, green rolled with the rolling wheels of buses red and green and cars full of people who were not surprising each other. Also dull sods, I thought.

Then I began to sing.

In my head I can sing like the greatest, like Callas, Los Angeles, like Jessye Norman and Flagstadt. In my head. In reality I have the voice of a crow. For heaven's sake I wasn't even allowed to sing in the choir in school.

'No, no, no, Stella Macnamara, we can't have you,' the music teacher would say.

'If you could sing quietly you could stay, but you will insist on shouting.'

Printemps qui commence,

A song for spring.

Portant l'espérance
Aux coeurs amoureux,

hat a voice.

Ton souffle qui passe
De la terre efface
Les jours malheureux.

81

We moved quicker now, spaces spreading between the cars.

Fewer Hore Belishas.

The star still constant.

Tout brûle en notre âme,
Et ta douce flamme
Vient sécher nos pleurs,
Tu rends à la terre,
Par un doux mystère,
Les fruits et les fleurs.

It gets a bit sad after that. There I will leave Delilah.

The hanging star had been joined by a million others when we drew up outside an old timbered building. Warm light from the door and windows fell onto the gravel.

He switched off the engine.

'Here we are.'

I opened the door and got out.

The smell was of countryside, damp grass and curling wood smoke.

'No moon,' I said. 'No sweet and lovely moon. I suppose you can't have everything.'

'I beg your pardon, madame.'

A man in shirt-sleeves and a green apron had materialised beside me.

'I'm sorry. I just talk to myself a lot.'

He leant into the car.

'If you wouldn't mind, sir, the car park is round to the left. I will take the bags in for you.'

Martyn had a neat little leather case. I had

an old brown holdall.

He bowed me into the hotel.

'Mrs ...?'

He put the bags on the floor and went behind a handsome table to where the keys hung in a box on the wall.

'Glover.'

He took down the remaining key and handed it to me.

'Thank you.'

'Will you wait for Mr Glover or will I show you to your room straight away?'

'I'll wait.'

We waited in silence.

A fire burned in a hooded grate, huge logs which conversed in murmurs as they were consumed, and murmurs also from a room on the right, where people were probably having their dinner.

I was ravenous.

*　　　*　　　*

'The birds.'

It was much later. We had eaten our dinner and drunk our wine and I had pulled the opulent velvet curtains in our room and opened the window and I was looking at the stars; Orion's Belt, the Great Bear, the Little Bear, the North Star, they were all satisfactorily in their places. Still no moon. It was the great wash of the Milky Way that illuminated the fields below us, the trees, the neat English hedges. I still didn't know where we were. East, that was all I knew.

'The birds,' he repeated.

He came across the room and put his arm round my shoulders.

'Why do we always have to have the window open?'

He whispered the words into my ear as if he were saying ... I love you, darling.

'What about the birds?'

'Did you honestly think it was a ... wonderful...'

He searched for a word.

'It was wonderful,' I said.

'A wonderful...'

He smiled deep into my eyes. I felt the touch of his smile down in my belly.

'A trick. I'd call it a trick.'

'Oh, no, no. Not that word. I am not a trickster.'

He pulled me away from the window towards the bed.

'It's not a trick. A trick is false. I have explained all this to you before, my Star. This was true, real. You saw two real birds. Two real men. You saw nothing that was unreal.'

'Fire in his hands? The birds flying out of the fire?'

He pushed me down into the pillows.

'It's how you choose to look that's
84

important. How you interpret what you see.'

'No. I have no choice.'

He was slowly unbuttoning my shirt, his fingers sliding over my skin.

'I have to look where you insist. That's the important thing, to look where you insist. That's where the trickery comes in. I have no choice.'

'Illusion.'

'I have no choice.'

'That's the way I want it to be. No choice.'

'At this moment, I love no choice.'

'I love.'

*   *   *

The house he took me to see the next morning was a charming red-brick gentleman's residence in good decorative condition with a gem of a mature garden and a large well-maintained barn.

A red-brick gentleman in good condition from a London house agency showed us round.

He flourished and jangled a bunch of keys with the expertise of a prison officer.

'Drawing-room.'

He ushered us into a room with long windows, full of blue and green sunstreaked light.

'Central heating.'

He opened and shut a door and we caught a

85

glimpse of a shining boiler.

'And wait till you see the kitchen, Mrs ... um ... Glover. Just you wait.'

Quarry-tiled floor and an oil-fired Aga. No expense spared. Handmade pine fittings and a double sink ... now quite commonplace, but almost unheard of then.

As we climbed the well-proportioned staircase to have a look at the bedrooms and two bathrooms, one *en suite*, I spoke my first words.

'Why did the owners feel they had to leave this ... paradise?'

'Isn't it? Isn't it just? Oh dear me, yes.'

He turned and flashed me a smile.

His teeth were very white. He must have a great dentist, I thought.

'Abroad. The lure of abroad. The youngest child out of school at last. They felt they could move away. Isn't it good to indulge yourself if you can? Yes. I say yes, all the time. They bought a charming place on the Côte d'Azur ... well a couple of miles up from the coast actually. Quite unspoiled. The firm managed the whole deal for them. Not me personally, you understand, but we do have a department that deals purely in foreign, mainly Mediterranean, properties. Yes. It's all starting to open up.'

He shook the keys and unlocked a door.

'Master bedroom.'

He hurried in ahead of us, opening doors

86

and cupboards, waving his hands at the view from the window.

'Bathroom, as I said, *en suite*, tiny dressing-room, built in ... as you see you could move in straight away. Carpets and curtains are up for offer. Some people prefer to make their own decisions about such things and then some people, yes, quite a number really, like the no problems ease of just taking what is already in place. Yes.'

He caught Martyn's eye.

'Whoever buys it could move straight ... quite. Charming bathroom, don't you think? I always think the bathroom is almost the most important ... Bidet. Brass taps. Very good water pressure, I have been told.'

God, I thought, my mother would hate this man.

He turned on a brass tap and water gushed out.

'See. Some people worry about water pressure. This is another no problem area here.'

He tweaked the tap off again.

'Coming from London where you have every amenity.'

'We're not thinking of leaving London and its amenities.'

He looked surprised and opened his mouth to say something, but Martyn forestalled him.

'May I see the barn?'

'Of course, of course. It's in tiptop shape.'

He set off after Martyn.

'We'll leave you to have a look around Mrs ... um. Open all the cupboards. You are free to explore fully. Ladies have their own point of view. I always find it a good thing to leave the lady on her own for a while ... And the garden...' He called the words back up as he rushed across the hall. 'The garden is a gem. Do step into the garden.'

I watched them from the bedroom window, winding their way across the grass, through the bushes and trees, just starting to come into tiny leaf. They nodded their heads towards each other like Chinese dolls. They were each wearing cavalry twills and brown tweed jackets. I longed for Martyn to reach out his hand towards the other man and conjure from his nostril or ear half a pound of Cadbury's Milk Tray, or maybe twenty Player's Navy Cut. I could imagine the alarm on the face of the house agent as the white cylinders plopped from his ear-hole.

Come into the garden Maud,
For the black bat night has flown.
Come into the garden Maud...

My mother's voice was rich and low.

She used to sing on winter evenings when the curtains were pulled tight. Richly she sang and accompanied herself and the sound of the notes flew out from under her firm fingers.

And the woodbine spices are wafted abroad,
And the musk of the rose is blown.
Maud was one of my father's favourites, and he would put his book down and listen to her and nod his head in time to the music.

I used to wonder what he was remembering. His own mother perhaps, also singing in the flickering firelight? The thought of such continuity is very potent.

I had no music in me.

She also used to sing Schubert.

Röslein, Röslein, Röslein, rot,
Röslein auf der Hei ... eiden.

I was all fingers and thumbs when it came to playing the piano.

'You must concentrate when you practise, Stella. Your mind is always a million miles away. You'll never get anywhere if you don't practise.'

She used to put her head round the schoolroom door and scold me ...

My brother John could thunder '*Für Elise*' at breakneck speed, but I could never get the fingering right. I suppose I didn't want to.

My mother always said you could do anything in the world you wanted, if you tried hard enough.

'Application,' she would say and leave me to ponder.

I will have to have a child to whom I can tell these silly things.

Some time or other.

'Star!'

Bird.

Birds in the high hall garden
When twilight was falling.

'Star. Star.'

Maud. Maud. Maud,
Were crying and calling.

'Wake up, Star.'

He was below me on the lawn, crying and calling. The house agent, keys in his hand, was standing beside him. Their upturned faces were pink and expectant. I raised a hand and waved.

A bit like the Queen, I thought.

A gracious wave.

'Come on down, for heaven's sake,' shouted Martyn.

He was rattling coins impatiently in his pocket when I came out of the door.

'What on earth were you doing, standing there like a loony? I shouted and shouted.'

The house agent moved towards me, his face was filled with understanding.

'Having a good sniff round? Yes, of course. I think you'll have found everything A.1. Isn't the bathroom suite a peach? I hope you found the linen cupboards on the back landing. Second to none those linen cupboards. Everything to your liking?'

'Yes, thank you.'

'A.1. We seldom get a property in such

90

perfect nick as this.'

'The barn is a dream,' said Martyn, taking a leaf from the agent's book.

'I don't doubt it. Well? What's next on the agenda? What other little surprises have you got in store for me?'

The house agent looked alarmed.

Martyn laughed.

'Don't pay any attention to her,' he said. 'Let's go and have a drink. I'm sure there's a pub somewhere.'

'There is. Yes, there is indeed. In the village, just a stone's throw away.' He looked at me and laughed nervously. 'That is, of course if you're quite good at throwing stones. Charming old hostelry. Charming village really, quite untouched by...'

'I think I'd like a drink,' I said.

* * *

'There were things I always used to wonder about your father.'

She has eaten everything I put before her. Her plate is as clean as if a dog had licked it. Her elbows are on the table, her head propped in her hands.

'Like what?'

'Tomorrow will do. After you've had a good night's sleep.'

She shakes her head.

91

'Now. Tomorrow you will make excuses. Escape.'

'Not at all.'

'Give me another glass of wine.'

She sits up straight and pushes her glass towards me across the table.

'Coffee?'

'I won't sleep. Just wine.'

I get up and open another bottle.

'Well?'

I pick up her glass and watch as the wine slides into it from the bottle, glowing, rich with signals from the candles.

I sigh.

'Well?' she says again.

I wonder whether to fill my own glass or not. Why the hell not?

'I always used to wonder where he came from. Who he came from. Who begat your father?'

'Curiosity killed the cat.'

'I've often wondered if he told you things that he never told me. Or took you somewhere and said ... I used to play in this street ... I used to walk on this stony beach. Did he ever speak his geography to you? Or his history? Who slapped him when he was a child? Who sang songs to him? What were the songs they sang?'

'It's a bit late to be asking these questions now. Why didn't you ask him when he was alive?'

'I did. Over and over again. He said it didn't matter.'

'He was right.'

She takes a long drink.

'He was right. He ... Martyn ...' her voice shakes as she says the name. 'Martyn didn't care about all those middle-class notions about the past. Influences, culture, roots. Romantic rubbish he said. The stuff novelists feed on. He always said that novelists were just gossips who knew how to use typewriters.'

'He would.'

'It's today and tomorrow that matter. Yesterday is for the dustbin. You have to work out what you want and go and get it.'

'Perhaps that's why the prisons of the western world are so full. They've all been to the same school as your father.'

'Don't be so bloody unkind.'

'I hope you don't agree with him.'

'I would like to carry no baggage ... be like him.'

'He carried two hundred white doves.'

'That was a rotten thing to say.'

'Yes, it was. I'm sorry.'

She clenches her hands into fists and for a moment I think that maybe she is going to hit me and I think that I probably deserve it.

We sat in silence until one of the candles begins to gutter. I stretch out a hand and squeeze the flame to death.

'You are a bitter old harridan.'

She gets up and leaves the room, leaving me with the washing up and half a bottle of wine.

* * *

We drove in silence back to the hotel.

He whistled through his teeth.

A nothing sound.

A warning sound.

Along the narrow country roads with hedges just starting to green and wide East Anglia fields and a shimmer of sun in a hazy sky.

I longed for whin bushes and the lace of dry-stone walls with the light shining through.

I thought, you stupid cow, you left. You chose. You kept choosing and anyway in Dublin there are no whins and no lacy stone walls, so fuck it, stop calling up these sentimental icons. Have sense, woman.

A trail of dust followed us up the avenue like smoke from the funnel of a train, and then settled gently once more.

I got out of the car and slammed the door.

I ran up the stairs to our room and began to collect my oddments and shove them into a holdall.

He came into the room and stood by the door.

'What are you doing?'

'What does it look like?'

94

'Please.'

'Please, what?'

He took a few steps into the room and stood so dejected, almost despairing, between me and the door.

'You must forgive me. Please. It was meant to be such a happy occasion.'

'What on earth do you mean, a happy occasion? You appear to be buying a house without talking to me about it. Without asking me what I thought.'

'I thought you'd love it. Isn't it a house in a million? The house of your dreams?'

'It depends on your dreams.'

'My dream is to have a house ... a real home ... with you, darling. With our children. A safe, lovely home. That's all I want. I am only safe with you, Star. Oh, Star.'

I sat down on the bed and let the holdall fall to the floor.

'I am so selfish.'

He moved across the room and knelt down at my feet.

'So selfish. I don't deserve to have someone like you.'

He laid his head in my lap. I could see his right eye, tears, like pearls, quivered on the lashes.

'I want to be everything in the world to you. I want no one in the world except you ... Say something, Star ... Please ... I'm so frightened

95

that I've destroyed everything.'

He rolled his head down into my lap and began to cry.

'I'm sorry,' I said.

I touched his hair. He'll be getting bald by the time he's forty, I thought. I wondered if his father had had that fragility, that scalp vulnerable to the sun.

'I'm sorry. Don't cry ... Please don't. We should have discussed this before, that's all.'

'I wanted it to be such a lovely ... gift. Something perfect for you ... The right setting for my jewel.'

He turned his head and looked up at me.

He put up a hand and touched my face.

'You don't understand, do you?'

'Perhaps not. You don't say much. I'm a bit of a plodder. I have to take things slowly.'

'I wasn't going to make any decisions. Nothing like that. I just wanted you to see it. If you don't like it, of course...'

'It's not that. It's a lovely house. But we have to talk about leaving London. We have to talk about my job, for God's sake. I never envisaged myself living in the country in England. I always thought it was London or nothing. I have my own countryside inside me ... I don't feel I need this. Couldn't we buy a house in London, if you want to buy a house? Notting Hill or Hampstead if you want to be surrounded by trees. What's wrong with that?'

'It's more than that. The barn here is

96

fabulous. I really need that sort of space if I want to get to work on my bird act.'

'Bird act? You haven't told me about a bird act either.'

'It may take years to get it right. I can't talk about it. It might just all crumble away if I talk about it. It will need space. A large studio and space for hundreds of doves. You can't find that in Notting Hill. The barn is as perfect as the house is. It was Rhodes who saw this place first and told me about it. He's been...'

He stopped abruptly.

He took my hand and began to stroke my fingers gently.

'We can build an aviary at the side of the barn. We can work there ...'

'Hang on a minute. Who is we?'

'Rhodes and Magill and myself. Maybe as time goes on we may have to call in more help, but I hope not. We want this to be our own personal miracle. Yes. Miracle. Do you understand?'

'You haven't given me much to go on.'

'Do you trust me?'

'Of course I trust you, darling.'

He let go of my hand and jumped to his feet.

He stood with his back to the window, a black silhouette, one hand stretched out towards me. The sun, which was now quite strong, shone through his thinning hair.

'It will be your decision. Only yours. I promise you if you say no, I will not argue. I am

97

in your hands.'

A flower began to grow in the palm of his outstretched hand.

I had been about to ask all the sensible questions that were in my head; the questions undoubtedly of someone with anxiety and no vision.

It was a camellia.

Someone who had sense, but no understanding of the needs of others.

Pink, double, with glossy leaves. He held it out towards me between his finger and thumb.

I put out my hand and took it from him.

'Thank you.'

'Anything, anything, my Star, you ever want.'

I nodded. As my head moved, I felt a tear sliding down my face.

He picked up my holdall from the floor and took the things from it, laying each one gently on the bed beside me.

'What an awful man,' he said. 'A creep. Isn't that what you would call him?'

I nodded again.

'Yes, he's a creep all right.'

He picked up the telephone.

'He may still be in the pub. I'll just give them a ring and see. You did say yes, didn't you?'

I nodded.

*   *   *

98

'Yes.'

My mother always answered the telephone so. There was never a welcoming sound to her voice. It was always as if you had disturbed her in the middle of some very important act.

'Mummy.'

'Ah. How are you, my dear?'

'I'm fine.'

'How's the weather over there?'

'Lovely.'

'Well? I presume you have some news?'

She waited for the news. I pictured her in her tweed coat and skirt holding the receiver, which always smelt faintly of Dettol, slightly away from her ear as she waited for whatever news it was.

News never happened to them at home. Life just went on. News was something that happened in other places.

'We're buying a house.'

There was a pause.

'What was that, dear?'

'We're buying a house.'

Another pause.

'Is that a very sudden decision? You've never mentioned such a thing before.'

'Pretty sudden, really.'

'Where? Somewhere nice, I hope. I hope you'll have a spare room, so that Daddy and I can come and stay.'

'Suffolk.'

'Suffolk! That's the country.'

99

'It's a lovely house. Sort of Queen Anne. On the edge of one of those picture postcard villages. A garden. You'll love it.'

'You don't know anything about gardening.'

'I can learn.'

There was a very long pause. I could hear her breathing as she thought about the news.

'How far is it from London? My geography is hopeless. What about your job? Are you going to become a commuter? Are you going to sit for hours on a train each day?'

'Martyn will do that all right. He thinks it's a cheap price to pay for living in such a lovely place. I...'

'I thought you were going to become a partner.'

'I've put that off for a while. I think I'll be domestic for a couple of years and then...'

She was laughing.

Damn.

'Mummy...'

'There's a fool born every minute. Lovely news, dear. I'll tell your father. This is costing.'

She put down the receiver.

Damn.

*　　*　　*

I get myself to bed, my head is muddled with too much wine and tiresome reincarnations.

My room has two long windows and light

100

from the street lamps quivers across the floor.

I like this.

I like the strips of light and dark, the faint illumining of familiar objects. I have never liked the dark. The stirring of inanimate objects in the dark has always troubled me. The curtains in this room are purely for decoration, except during thunderstorms when I pull them tight and jump into bed and cover my head with the bedclothes. Even then I imagine I can see the flashes splitting through my closed eyes.

As a rule I don't notice dreams, but since Martyn's death last week, I have been dreaming of birds; patterns of birds on a huge sky, motionless and yet seeming to move inexorably towards me. Trees, covered with feathers, instead of leaves, rustling slightly as the breeze brushes them against each other. In one dream I bent down to pick something from my bedroom floor and my hand touched a dead, white dove, still warm, but quite surely dead. I was frightened by the feel of my fingers sinking through the feathers and woke up to feel my heart thundering.

'Jesus, I hate you Martyn,' I said aloud to myself and then was sorry, it seemed such an uncouth thing to say.

'It will be all right tomorrow. Just you wait and see.'

She used to say that.

After Our Father.

After Now I lay me down to sleep.
After God bless Mummy and Daddy.
She would kiss me.

She always smelt the same; lily of the valley, that was her permanent smell. Nowadays mothers are more exotic.

Kiss me and say 'It will be all right tomorrow'.

Nowadays I just take a short cut, cut the crap, just fall into sleep, winding through misty thoughts, singing in my head.

Your feets too big.
Don't want you 'cos your feets too big.

No birds tonight, please. I've enough on my plate without birds to battle with.

Don't like you 'cos your feets too big.
I hate you 'cos your feets too big.
La deedada.
La deedada...

And of course I know it won't be all right tomorrow.

* * *

'You're sure this is what you want?'

He seldom had to leave for work as early as I did and he stood that morning in the hall, wrapped in a bath towel. Steam rose from his body, as mist lifts from the summer fields on a warm morning.

I looked at him for a moment and then

opened the hall door.

'Yes,' I said.

I had said those words so many times in the preceding twenty-four hours that I was now beginning to accept them as truth.

'You're looking very smart.'

'Thank you. I'm having lunch with Bill. This is the day ... you know ... I have to tell him that I ... I thought I ought to look a bit tidy. He takes his lunches quite seriously.'

He rubbed at his wet hair with a hand.

'What are you going to say to him?'

'I'll say that we're moving out of London. There's not much else to say. Things shift all the time. That's the ...'

'What a pity I've never met him.'

'You always said no, when I suggested having him to dinner.'

'Did I? I don't remember. Can't stand intellectuals. Can't stand snobs. Have a good lunch. Don't forget me.'

I laughed at such a thought and went to work.

* * *

We had lunch at the White Tower.

Martyn was right. The restaurant was filled with intellectuals and what he definitely would have called snobs. A discreet buzz of gossip, deals, chat, laughter, more gossip, filled the room.

We had a glass of wine, discussed the menu, chose our meal and then I told Bill that I would not be accepting his offer of a partnership; that I would, in fact, be leaving the office quite soon. My voice was matter of fact, quite calm. He listened without interrupting me, a courtesy, I had noticed, that he gave to all his writers. From time to time he lifted his wineglass to his lips. The wine was cold and the outside of the glass had a mist on it. When I stopped talking he looked at me for a few moments in silence before he spoke.

'Bloody women. Always let you down.'

'I'm sorry.'

He laughed.

'I shouldn't have said that, but I had a bit of a battle with the board about this. They're a somewhat prejudiced lot. I'm trying to kick them into this century. Yes, quite prejudiced, fuddy duddy, in spite of some of the books we publish ... *C'est la vie*, sport. I was looking forward to working with you. I thought we might get on well, I like the channels through which your mind wanders.'

A waiter put a plate of stuffed vine leaves in front of me and filled my glass.

'Bloody women.'

'I'm sorry.'

'We're seriously repeating ourselves. I take it you've thought this through. I don't see you as the sort of woman who plays hard to get games.'

'I was so pleased ... yes, I've thought it through.'

He scooped some taramasalata onto a piece of toast.

'Tell me about this man, husband, the chap in your life. Apart from wanting to do bizarre things with birds. I mean to say, what does he do with his life, sport? To be crude, how does he earn a crust?'

I didn't say anything.

'Sport?'

'I don't know. This makes me seem very foolish. I know that. He goes to an office every day. He has a secretary called Angela. He has a partner, whose name I have forgotten. I have asked so many questions and I receive no answers.'

'Sleeping with Angela?'

'I shouldn't think so.'

'Why the secrecy then?'

'Import, export, is all he says.'

He giggled.

'Rubber goods to the Indians? French letters? Dutch caps?'

'He keeps his lips buttoned.'

'How frustrating. Where did you find him?'

'On a train. He's OK Bill. Honestly he is. He's just superhumanly discreet.'

'There's lots of money in rubber goods. He seems to have lots of money. What's his family like? Do you have trouble with the mother-in-law?'

I shook my head.

He had taramasalata sticking to the side of his mouth. He wiped at it with his napkin.

'You're mad,' he said. 'Insane. Here I was thinking you were a bright lady. Straightforward and very probably creative, now I know you're mad.'

'You're behaving like my mother. He's a wonderful man. I love him.'

'Forgive me, Stella. Please, please forgive me. I'm used to people being more practical than you are, more orderly. I really hope that you will be very happy.'

'Yes. I think that's what all this is about. Ultimate happiness. Achieving dreams. Someone's got to give.'

'You? How do you choose?'

He put another heap of taramasalata into his mouth.

'Perhaps becoming a publisher is not all that important.'

'Thanks.'

'For me.'

'And perhaps dreaming of being the world's greatest conjuror is?'

'Illusionist. At least it's something. I only know that I don't have much of a dream at the moment and he has. So, there we are.'

'In Suffolk.'

'For the time being.'

Our plates were removed and more wine was poured.

106

At the far end of the restaurant a man laughed loudly. Bill peered over my head to see who it was.

Plates of fragrant lamb stew with apricots were put in front of us.

I picked up my fork and Bill put a hand across the table and touched my fingers.

'We'll miss you in the office, sport.'

'Thanks.'

'Pity. I really wanted a partner from within. I want to build an image, you know. It's always so boring pinching likely lads from other firms.'

'Or lasses.'

'Not on your nelly. I'm not going through this again for a while. We will remain a bastion of male chauvinism for years to come. See what you've done.'

He took a forkful of stew and spilled a lot of it on his tie.

'Damn!'

He rubbed at his tie with his napkin.

'I never seem to be able to eat a meal without getting it over myself.'

'You should tuck your napkin into your collar, like the French.'

'My mother would disown me and I'm sure I'd be asked to resign from the club. I'm not sure what you mean by achieving happiness. Talk to me about happiness. Are you sure such a thing exists?'

'The Americans think so. Aren't they

exhorted to pursue it?'

He laughed and waved his dirty napkin at me.

'Pish, sport, that won't do at all. I do like you, Stella. I think you have ability, humour, a bit of magic really. I want to know why...'

Something made me look up to find Martyn standing by our table. He smiled at me.

I blushed.

'... you want to...'

'What on earth are you doing here?'

'The same as you. Having lunch. What a strange coincidence.'

'I didn't know you ate in Soho.'

'I eat all over the place. Won't you introduce me...?'

'Bill Freeman.' Bill put out a hand as he spoke. 'I suppose you're Mr Glover.'

They touched hands, rather than shook.

'Great to meet you,' said Martyn. 'After so long. Strange meeting you both like this.'

'Well, this is the office canteen really. I was just telling Stella how sorry I am that she is leaving us. Will you join us?'

'No thanks. I'm with someone. I won't disturb you any longer. I just felt I had to say hello. Hello, Star.'

'Hello,' I said.

'Goodbye.' He bowed slightly to us both.

'Goodbye,' we both said at once.

He turned and walked to the back of the restaurant. I watched him every step of the

108

way. He knew I was watching him. He sat down with his back to us at a table where a small, dark man was carefully reading the menu.

'Hmmm,' said Bill.

He picked up his pudding spoon and began to shovel stew into his mouth.

'What does hmmm mean?'

'Whatever you want it to mean, sport.'

'You don't have to like him. You don't have to have any feelings about him at all.'

'I'm just amused, that's all. His friend is staring at me over the top of his menu.'

'Don't look, Bill. Pretend they're not there.'

'My eyes are drawn as if by magnets. Mittel European, I think.'

He picked up a piece of bread and ran it round his plate, gathering up golden juice.

'God, this is good. Tell you something, if I weren't a publisher, I think I'd own a restaurant. I just love food. Do you think he thinks we're having an affair? May I hold your hand?'

He put the bread into his mouth and held his hand out across the table to me. I ignored it.

'There's one thing I'd like to say. Stella, are you listening?'

I nodded.

'It has occurred to me over the last couple of months and I think this is the time to mention it. Have you ever thought that you might be a writer?'

'No.'

'Well, when you're sitting in Suffolk watching the daisies grow and wondering where your husband is or who he is...'

'Shut up, Bill. I hate the silly sneers you come out with sometimes.'

'Not sneers, sport. No. Don't go. Please don't get up and leave in high dudgeon. We're going to have pudding ... and brandy. You owe it to me. You've just thrown a spanner in my plans. I'm going to have baklava and then goat's cheese and then brandy and coffee. You can watch me or join me. But we're going to sit them out. Right, sport?'

'Amen.'

'There's my girl.'

He waved exuberantly at the waiter.

'Have baklava. It's so sticky you can actually feel your teeth rotting as you chew. Divine.'

We had baklava and goat's cheese and just as we ordered our coffee and brandy, Martyn and the dark man passed us without acknowledgement and went out into the street.

'Rubber goods or guns?'

'Do shut up,' I said to him. But I did wonder myself.

*   *   *

It's never all right tomorrow.

I sometimes used to wonder what was wrong

110

in her life that she had to say those words evening after evening.

Around her everything seemed so pleasant, so orderly.

Were there dark secrets in her head?

Were there secrets that couldn't be spoken? Even to the people she loved?

But of course those are the people from whom we keep our secrets.

They are the people who can destroy our dreams.

Probably, though, she just felt the need to protect me in some way from the future, clear a path for me by murmuring her mantra, spell, prayer, incantation.

I can hear Robin in the kitchen turning on the tap and filling the kettle. I can hear the murmur of the radio.

When you live alone your ears pick up very quickly the alien sounds that happen when someone else enters your space.

I hear the milkman each morning as I unwrap myself from sleep, the rhythmic jingle of the bottles as he walks up the path to the door, the clink as he puts each one in its place. Two for the O'Hagans, one for Mrs Meaney on the top floor, three and always a large cream for the Henrys. He scoops up the empties and rattles quickly to the gate, which squeals as he closes it behind him. I don't get milk from the milkman as I live alone and my consumption of milk is minimal and erratic. I also hear the postman. In fact I wait with anticipation to hear the slithering sound the letters make as they fall to the floor in the hall. I lie in bed each day and listen to this overture with great contentment.

If Robin were not here I would get up now and prepare myself for my working hours, breakfast, bath, dress, read my post, listen to the awful news on the radio and wish that I cared more. Somewhere else is so far away. From the morning warmth of my bed everywhere outside this room is somewhere else.

Perhaps she'll bring me a cup of tea.

Perhaps she will open the door cautiously, putting her head around it to see if I am awake or asleep before coming into the room, the steaming cup held out in front of her.

I would welcome that intimacy.

That unthreatening intimacy.

*   *   *

Every morning at seven thirty I used to hear Molly cross the landing with two cups of tea on a tray for my mother and father. I would hear her open their bedroom door and the low murmur of voices as she gave them a weather report and the rattle of the curtains as she pulled them back to let in the day. She would come out of their room and cross the landing to bang on my door.

'*Awake,*' she would shout, '*for morning in the bowl of light...*'

She would pass down the passage to my brothers' doors.

'*... has flung the stone that puts the stars to flight.*'

No laggards were allowed. No lieabeds.

Her teacher must have been a person of vast and catholic tastes as Molly seemed to have a quotation for almost every eventuality, from Shakespeare to Tom Moore, from Tennyson and Dickens to Oscar Wilde. She seemed to have them all at her command.

*　　*　　*

The door opens.

There is a little sigh as it moves over the carpet.

Robin puts her head around the door.

'A cup of tea?'

'Lovely, darling.'

Her head disappears and I sit up pummelling at my pillows, so that I can lie back into them in a position fit for drinking tea.

She comes into the room with the steaming cup held out in front of her. She is wearing an old dressing-gown of mine, navy blue cotton, with white spots. Her feet are bare. She doesn't look refreshed by sleep. She puts the tea down on my bedside table and stands looking at me. Her eyes are rimmed with red.

113

'Did you sleep . . .?'

We both stop speaking at the same time. She gives a nervous laugh.

'Snap,' she says.

I wait for a moment to see whether she will answer the question we both asked.

'Nightmares.'

She sits down on the bed and gropes in her pocket for her cigarettes. She shoves one in her mouth and clicks at her lighter until a flame comes. She stares at the light, as if surprised to see it, the cigarette balancing between the first and second fingers of her left hand. She clicks the flame off and puts the lighter back in her pocket.

'Sorry.'

'Sorry what?'

'I shouldn't smoke in your bedroom.'

'These are extenuating circumstances. Puff away, if you want to.'

She smiles slightly and puts the cigarette back in its packet.

'Yes, I suppose they are. Did you sleep?'

'On and off. I had recollections rather than nightmares. Nothing too fearful, I'm glad to say.'

'Can I ask you something?'

'I'm sure you can.'

She frowns.

'I mean, may I?'

'Anything. I may not be able to answer, but I promise I'll do my best.'

114

I think I know what she is going to ask me.

'He loved you very much.'

Oh God! Wrong again … This is a maze through which I really cannot see my way.

I wait.

What else is there for me to do?

I take a drink of tea.

She sits and stares at me, still holding the cigarette packet in her hand.

'That's not a question,' I say at last. 'And I don't even think it's a true statement of fact.'

She remains silent.

She is pointing the packet at me, as if it were a gun.

'Your father loved himself. Deeply. And you. I do believe he loved you. Look, Robin, there's no point in you trying to make me feel guilty about your father. I never did and I never will. I'm truly sorry he died the way he did; that was a grotesque and horrible end. No one deserves such an end. But, if he cried and wailed and beat his breast to you about me, then he was telling you lies, as he told me lies, as he told everyone lies. I think you should bear that in mind.'

She stands up abruptly.

'I don't know why I came.'

'For comfort.'

'A fat lot of that I'm getting.'

'Well, at least you had a good meal.'

Suddenly she throws the cigarette packet across the room. It lands with a silly plop, just inside the door. She runs after it, my dressing-gown flowing behind her.

'I really hate you. I can't bear your stupid jokes … can't bear …'

She bends and picks up the packet. She has good legs, I think, as I watch her. Good, long legs. Good narrow feet. At least she's got something from me.

'… your way of carrying on. Sorry.'

She speaks the last word abruptly and goes out of the room, closing the door behind her.

I wonder what she is sorry about; perhaps her use of that word, hate.

Perhaps not.

Is she packing her bag?

Perhaps she has tried to love me and failed?

Perhaps not.

I am not unlovable; at least, I don't think I am.

What I did was to protect myself; my integrity, if that's not too grandiose a word, my being.

Vows and promises should be approached with caution, not, I think, in the heat of passion.

Perhaps another name for passion could be foolishness, which brings me back to my mother.

I truly didn't hate my mother.

I was exasperated by her.

I loathed her propensity for so often being right.

I despised her complacency.

I couldn't have lived with her, under the one roof, even in, I thought at the time, the one city. But after I ran, I couldn't get her out of my head. I heard her voice constantly in my head. I would shake my head to dislodge her voice and the words would scatter like a flock of birds disturbed and then they would reassemble themselves again, floating on the pale breeze of my thoughts.

I felt persecuted by her.

I never hated her.

I never use that word in my thoughts about her. Even if I had, I would never have used that word to her face. I never used any of these words to her face. I just ran.

And now they have become my children, she and my father and Molly, of course. I long to protect them from all the dangers that I see around, not just the violence in the streets, the glue sniffers on the pier as the light thickens, but the sorrow and rage of the dispossessed, the violated, the disregarded cries of people without hope. I would love them to move quietly to their deaths still full of most of the certainties for which I used to despise them.

Good conquers evil.

God is love.

God is on our side.

God is.

My prayer for the dying.

Save them from knowledge o Lord!

117

When I offer to drive them in the evenings to their bridge parties or dinner with friends, trips to the National Concert Hall, she laughs, amused.

'We can manage, dear. If we can't manage, I'll let you know.'

She rebuked me once.

'We do love to see you, dear, but we don't want you to fuss.'

The word fuss was like a snake, slithering out of her mouth.

She has turned on the radio. I can hear BBC early tones coming from the kitchen.

Thought for the Day.

Interviews with Junior Ministers.

Loranorder.

I wonder will they ever catch the people who blew Martyn out of the world without even hating him, without even knowing his name.

I probably didn't know his name.

Does Robin know his name?

Does it bloody well matter?

*　　*　　*

I was able to hear the doves from my bed on summer mornings. About five o'clock the first sleepy murmurs would start from the aviary that Martyn had built behind the barn. I have always been an early waker, so the sounds never bothered me. I would just lie there, watching the sky turn blue. The first summer

118

there were only about fifteen of them and their early morning conversations were gentle and soothing, almost humorous they sounded as they chuckled and cooed and the baby inside me drummed with its feet or fists, a comfortable feeling that coincided each morning with the awakening of the doves.

One morning I was surprised by silence.

I lay for a long time wondering what was different; the baby cavorted, the tree and hedge birds in the garden were waking and trying out their voices, but there was no sound from the doves.

'Martyn.'

He used to sleep rolled up in a tight ball, his knees drawn up close to his chest, rather like a jockey.

'Martyn.'

I got out of bed and went over to the window and put my head out into the cool morning air.

'Martyn.'

'Ummm?'

He stretched out but didn't open his eyes.

'There's something wrong with the doves.'

'What do you mean? What time is it? For God's sake Star, come back to bed.'

'I can't hear them.'

'What do you mean, you can't hear them?'

He opened his eyes and looked first at his watch and then at me.

'It's half past five,' he said crossly.

'I can always hear them. There must be

119

something wrong.'

'They're just sleeping late. I hate the early morning.'

He rolled himself up again and pulled the bedclothes over his head.

I stood by the window for a few minutes listening to the doveless morning and watching the mist lifting off the grass and in the distance the sharp, triumphant bark of a fox and then I went downstairs and made myself a cup of tea.

I was reading greedily in those days; those light mornings and long summer evenings when perhaps Martyn didn't come home. During the body of the day I minded the house, wandering with astonishment through the empty rooms, admiring the way the light fell on polished wood and painted walls. I would crawl through the flower beds pulling up weeds, trying to learn and remember the names of flowers and shrubs. It never seemed to rain that summer: grasshoppers ticked in the meadow grass and I would walk in the afternoons along the winding roads trying to acquaint myself with this alien landscape, well-ditched fields stretching as far as the eye could see, near copses and a huge, cloudless sky, pale around the edges of the land and deepening as it rose above the earth to a powerful almost violent blue. Summer was summer here and no mistake.

I heard his footsteps in the room above and then the sound of water running into the bath, gurgling amicably into the pipes. I put down my book and went into the kitchen to make breakfast.

He liked the works; fried eggs, bacon, sausages, toast, coffee.

'I never know when I'll get my next meal,' he used to say.

He came into the kitchen and walked across the room and out of the back door without speaking a word. His feet left tracks in the damp grass. He was hardly gone two minutes before I heard the cry.

'Star.'

It was more like a scream, really.

'Star.'

I ran out across the damp, cold grass, through the rhododendrons and the azaleas, through their petals scattered on the grass, and round behind the barn to where he had built the aviary.

He stood by the netting, by a neat hole torn just above the low wall and stared through it at the dead bodies of ten or eleven white doves.

His face was white also, with anger and shock.

He gestured at the bodies with his hand.

He didn't say a word.

We stood in silence and I thought, poor dead things, necks neatly broken, as if by a professional.

There were some feathers on the grass near my bare foot, some footprints in the dew.

John, John, the grey goose is gone.
I remembered my mother used to sing it to me.

'Who would have done this?' He whispered the words. 'Who? Why?'

'No one, darling.'

'My birds. Why would anyone ...?'

And the fox to his lair in the morning.

She used to sing it with such gusto, rattling out the cheerful tune with her fingers.

'A fox.'

'Don't be silly. It must have been a man with pliers. Look at that hole.'

'A fox. Look.'

I pointed to the feathers and the tracks across the grass into the ditch and then gone.

To his lair in the morning.

'He barked,' I said.

'What do you mean?'

'I heard him bark when I looked out of the window, from way across the fields. Over there.'

He turned to me, his face raging, his eyes were stone at that moment.

'Why didn't you tell me?'

'But I did, darling. I woke you. I said ...'

'I know what you said. That's not what I mean. Why didn't you tell me about foxes?'

*   *   *

The doorbell rings.

Who, at this hour, could be ringing my doorbell?

I lie and wonder for a moment, before reaching for my dressing-gown and hitting the floor.

I am too slow.

I hear Robin's voice in the hall.

Surprised.

Welcoming.

The door closes.

A little laugh.

Mother's voice. 'Stella, dear. It's me.'

I hear their feet on the floor in the hall.

My mother always wears trim, high-heeled shoes, probably Italian. She has always had her vanities.

'I'll be with you in a minute.'

'No rush, dear. I've come to see the child.'

Then, a little laugh from Robin and they go into the kitchen and shut the door.

I may as well have a bath.

I may as well give them some space.

*   *   *

The aviary was reinforced, reconstructed, made impregnable to foxes.

Two young men from the village spent several days on the job.

They were quite taciturn.

I gave them cups of tea and chocolate biscuits. They thanked me and carried the cups over to the barn, later they brought back the empty cups and they thanked me again. I learnt nothing from them, except for their names, which I have forgotten...

Dr Rhodes and Peter Magill arrived the following weekend. They didn't come into the house; they arrived in the local taxi and I watched them from the window as they walked with Martyn across the grass. They went into the aviary and the few remaining doves scattered into the air in alarm.

I watched as they touched the wire mesh. One of them shook the upright pole that was one of the supports of the structure. They inspected the brickwork and the doves fluttered above their heads as they talked and nodded. They seemed quite content with the repair work.

Something seemed to split inside me, a feeling for a moment like fingers tearing at my gut.

How do you know...?

Then normality again.

First time, how do you ...?

I went across the room and picked up the telephone.

My hands were shaking as I dialled.

'Hello.'

'Molly.'

'She's in the garden.'

'Would you give her a shout, Molly, please.'

'You're two weeks early. Have the waters

124

broken or something?'

'I need to talk to her.'

'Are you starting off?'

'I ... No. I don't know.'

'She has visitors to tea.'

'Please.'

'I'll call out to her.'

My mother's voice was fretful when she arrived.

'What is this about? The Beresfords are here to tea.'

'I had this pain ...'

'One pain?'

'Yes ... but ...'

'Is whatsisname there?'

'Yes.'

'That's all right then. This is costing. Give me a ring when you're on your way and ...'

'Mummy ...'

'... for heaven's sake don't fuss.'

She put down the receiver.

I sat down and began to laugh.

The baby made no more alarming moves for two weeks.

She arrived on schedule.

*　　*　　*

I lie in the bath for a long time, not just out of tact, though there was an element of that, but because I love baths. I love the mild steaminess of bathrooms, the soft embracing of the body and limbs, for a few moments the world seems perfect. As the warmth creeps up your back, as water shimmers on your skin, dead thoughts as well as dead skin slough away. Yesterday's scum gathers on the surface of the water. Today I will wash my hair. I will give them time to recognise each other.

When I go into the kitchen after about half an hour, they look at me with astonishment, as if they had totally forgotten my existence.

Who is this woman, their faces seem to say.

My mother sits upright, orderly in the high-backed chair, her feet in her highly polished shoes positioned neatly side by side beneath the table. My daughter leans, her elbows on the table, an overflowing ashtray in front of her, smoke drifts from her mouth.

I feel I am about to be engulfed by a huge soppy wave of love.

'You needn't have rushed,' says my mother.

I laugh.

'Coffee? Tea? Anything, anyone?'

'Robin looks peaky,' says my mother. 'I told her she should take better care of herself. London is such an unhealthy place to live. No thank you, dear. I must go. I mustn't keep your father waiting.'

'Coffee,' says Robin.

'Where is he?'

She looks vague and doesn't answer.

'Mother! You haven't left him sitting outside in the car?'

126

'Just for a few minutes.'

She stands up.

'It's been over half an hour.'

'He's quite happy. He has *The Times*. He won't have noticed the time passing. He likes to read every word. I wanted to talk to the child alone. He understands these things you know, dear. He prefers to let me handle these things on my own.'

She leans forward and kisses Robin's cheek. Robin leans her head for a moment on her shoulder.

My mother looks bleached, opaque, every vestige of colour almost gone.

Robin looks like Martyn.

He will be back, I think, from beyond the grave. He has to have one last trick up his sleeve.

'Quarter to one. Don't be late. Your grandfather...'

'I won't be late,' says Robin.

'I'm not asking you, dear. I know you never go out to lunch.'

I nod meekly as she leaves the room.

*   *   *

Mother was there to greet me when I came home from the hospital with the baby.

Martyn had got twenty-four new doves while I had been away and the garden was filled with the sound of their murmuring.

127

We had tea outside, the baby in her pram under a tree and the dove sound around us.

My mother said little.

Martyn wandered over from time to time to look at the child.

'Who does she look like?' my mother called over to him.

He appeared not to hear.

She gathered the teacups onto the tray and carried it into the kitchen.

'How long is she going to stay?'

'She's only just come. Not long, darling...'

'I just want us to be alone.'

'Just till I...'

He bent and picked the baby out of the pram.

'She looks like a little bird. I think we'll call her Robin. Mrs Macnamara.' He called her name out loud. 'We've decided to call the baby Robin. I do hope you approve. She approves. She is smiling.'

'Wind,' said my mother, coming out into the garden once more. She walked across the grass. It was freshly cut and little threads of green clung to her shoes.

'At that age, it's always wind.'

He looked at her as if he didn't believe her.

'They can't see, you know, like kittens.'

She looked at the baby in his arms.

'She must take after your side. I thought her names were Emily Marion. That's what you said earlier.'

He handed the bundle to her.

'I have no side, Mrs Macnamara, so I couldn't possibly say.'

'You sprang like Venus, naked and unashamed from a scallop shell?'

His face was blank, his eyes a very pale grey as he looked at her. Luckily, Robin, with remarkable tact, began to cry.

I got up from the deckchair and went towards them.

'She's hungry.'

I took her from Mother.

Her tongue quivered alarmingly inside her wide open mouth, her unseeing eyes were blue slits.

'I'll see to her bottle.' Mother moved towards the house. 'It won't hurt her to cry for a few minutes.'

She disappeared.

Martyn looked after her.

'Don't mind her,' I said. 'She's only pulling your leg.'

He turned abruptly and walked towards the barn.

*   *   *

The fox came back.

I saw him one morning from Robin's window.

It was just after the early morning feed, about half-past six. After a clear and almost frosty night the sky was beginning to colour. I stood by the window with the baby against my shoulder, curled almost into sleep and I saw him, tail stretched behind him, trotting complacently through the bushes. He didn't look like a villain.

I didn't breathe a word to Martyn. I just kept my fingers crossed that the aviary was now fox proof. I liked the thought of him slipping in and out of our orderly life, leaving his tracks on the wet grass.

He was my first secret.

The night after my mother went home to Dublin, Martyn arrived back on the early train.

I had just finished putting the baby to bed when I heard him opening the hall door.

'Star,' he called from the hall.

I went to the top of the stairs and looked down. He was standing looking up at me, his arms filled with flowers.

I ran down to him and he threw his arms and the flowers around me and we kissed, kisses smelling of roses and lilies and stephanotis.

'How perfect,' he said. 'How wonderful to be alone.'

I disentangled myself from his arms and the flowers.

'She's not as bad as you think.'

'She doesn't like me. Every second that she was in this house, I could feel her despising me.'

I laughed a little uncomfortably.

130

'She just doesn't understand you. She really only likes what she can understand. She's very old-fashioned.'

'I don't like being despised in my own house.'

'Lovely flowers, my darling. I'll put them in water.'

I gathered them up and brought them into the kitchen.

As I busied myself with water and vases I stared out into the quiet country dusk. I was always hoping to catch a random sight of the fox.

'Star.'

He called me from the hall.

I dried my hands and went to him. There was no one in the hall.

'Star.'

The dining-room door was open and I went in. He had closed the curtains tight and was standing by the table waiting for me.

'We'll eat in here tonight. We'll celebrate.'

He held his hands out towards me. Two lighted candles suddenly began to grow and glow in his palms.

I clapped.

He handed them to me.

Red candles, the flames trembling.

He turned his back to me and stretched out his arms, two more candles appeared.

He turned towards me once more, the trembling lights reflected in his eyes.

'Candlelit dinner.' He put the two candles down on the table.

He stood for a moment, his hands clasped as if he were in prayer and then raising his hands above his head he let loose a bird into the air.

I screamed.

It flew up to the dark ceiling and finding no freedom there, swooped down towards the light. I dropped the two candles and ran out of the room, my hands covering my face. I ran into the kitchen and shut the door.

I stood in the middle of the floor, my heart throbbing and tears of fright and anger running down my face.

After a few minutes I heard him at the door.

'Don't come in. Don't let it ... please, don't.'

He opened the door and came in.

He held the dove in one hand against his chest.

I backed away from him.

'Don't ...'

'You are stupid. I'm not going to do anything. I thought you'd be ...'

'Nothing. Nothing. Just take it out of here now. You know I can't bear them.'

'You should try to bear them. They're perfectly harmless.'

He held the bird out towards me. It stared at me in an unfriendly way.

'Try,' he said.

He stroked the top of its head with a finger.

'Take it out, Martyn. Please.'

'I thought you were an intelligent woman.'

'I am an intelligent woman who hates birds. Get the hell out of here with that thing or...'

He left the room. I heard him cross the hall and open the front door. I heard him close the door behind him.

I walked into the dining-room and picked up the candles from the floor. I put them on the table beside the other two which were still burning. Little trails of red wax ran down their sides onto the table.

When Martyn eventually came back into the house, we ate our meal in a painful silence.

*   *   *

He gave me everything I ever needed.

My mother never came to our house again, but Robin and I would spend two or three weeks each year in Dublin.

I became a stranger in my own country. This was something I hadn't reckoned with. It was quite a painful estrangement.

I also was a stranger in the village.

I had acquaintances all right, people to whom I chatted in the street, people who invited us to dinner and who came to our house for meals. Decent enough people. Just not my people.

No man is an island, entire of itself.

There were times, Mr John Donne, when I would have shouted my disagreement at you.

133

Had you appeared.

Had you said those words to me in person.

I continued to get up at half-past six in the morning, even after I was finished with the early morning feed, even in the dark winter mornings, when all I could see when I looked out through the window was my own pale face mirrored in the dark window.

I woke one morning to feel that strange stillness that snow brings when it wraps the world. I stood by the window peering out at the pristine world as it coloured gradually, taking on first grey and then a pink glow as the sun began to push up behind the distant rim of the earth.

He came out of the shadows, his tail stretched out behind him and trotted across the lawn, leaving a trail clear and tempting, as he went.

I ran downstairs and threw a coat over my nightdress and pulled on my gumboots.

Outside the air was bitter, a sharp little wind blowing from the east.

I ran round the house, crunching my boots into the snow, and followed his trail.

And the fox to his lair in the morning.

Across the fields we went, up behind the village. Some lights were on, throwing their patterns onto the snow, but he and I were the only living things on the move.

I could no longer see him, but I imagined I could smell his feisty scent blowing back to me across the snow. I ran, clutching my coat around me, my boots sinking into the snow up to the ankles and then I lost him. He must have run along a ditch at the edge of a little wood and then under a ragged hedge, bowed down with the unaccustomed weight of the snow, and his tracks disappeared.

I stood for a while, quite silent, in the hope that he might signal in some way as to where he might be.

Of course he didn't and after a while I began to feel cold and quite foolish. I turned for home, hoping that I wouldn't meet anyone on the way.

The sun was above the horizon now and mist drifted in the air. One minute the village was visible over to the left, the next it was gone, as if it had been a mirage.

When I got back to the house Martyn was in the kitchen feeding cornflakes to Robin who was sitting at the table in her high-chair.

'Where in the name of God have you been?'

I pulled off my boots and put them by the stove.

My feet were frozen; next time I would pause long enough to put on socks.

'Star!'

'Mama,' said Robin, like one of those teddy bears that squeak when you turn them over.

'Where have you been?'

'I just felt like going for a walk.'

'You're mad.'

'The snow is so lovely when it's all fresh like that. No people to mess it up.'

'Here.' He handed me the spoon. 'You deal with the child. I'll probably miss my train.'

'You never said you were getting the early one.'

'Well, I am. Or was. You're usually so reliable. I haven't even had any breakfast.'

He left the room.

'I'll make you some now.'

'Don't bother. I've no time.'

His feet ran up the stairs.

I handed the spoon to Robin, who began to splash milk and cornflakes around the place. The kettle was whispering on the stove.

I took the teapot from the shelf and poured water into it and stood warming my hands on the brown china pot.

'Mama.'

'Yes, darling.'

I threw the water into the sink and put a teabag into the pot.

'Mama.'

My mother never used teabags.

'Mama.'

I poured boiling water into the pot.

'Mama.'

'Yes, darling.'

It was the sort of conversation we had for most of her waking hours.

'Mama.'

'Snow,' I said, turning and smiling at her.

'Lovely snow.'

I heard the hall door slam and after a moment or two the sound of his car revving up and then driving away.

Robin threw her spoon onto the floor.

'Snow,' she said as I bent down to pick it up.

* * *

I haven't thought about that fox for many years.

I gave him a name.

Guy.

Guy Fox.

Not a very good joke really, but it pleased me at the time.

I used to tell Robin stories about him.

'Once upon a time there was this fox called Guy...'

'What's called?'

'His name was Guy. Your name is Robin. My name is ...?'

'Mummystar.'

He brought her presents.

Each evening when he came home there was something in his pocket or up his sleeve; a rain of Smarties falling around her as she scrambled to catch them, or pick them up from the floor; glove puppets greeting her from his fingers, speaking her name as if they were old friends; fluffy dogs barked from inside his pocket and then leapt without effort or help into his arms.

137

Like me she had everything she wanted.

He never gave her a fox.

I used to wheel her across the fields in her push-chair, bumping over the grass until we came to the little wood and the hedge and I would tell her more stories about Guy Fox, about his lair and his night-time habits, about his cubs and the vixen guarding them from harm.

We found signs and signals, the strong smell that made her wrinkle up her nose with distaste; a few chewed bones, or feathers caught in the undergrowth looking as if they were growing from the untidy branches. I was always certain that he knew we were there, that he watched with his suspicious yellow eyes as the child and I wandered through the trees, or laid a rug on the grass and drank lemonade through straws out of a big glass bottle.

I knew his yellow eyes were watching.

Sometimes in the evening before the doves went to roost in the barn and the door was closed I would hear a wild fluttering in the aviary and the anxious calls of distressed birds and I would know that he had been around, staring at them perhaps through the netting, smiling a savage smile, his tongue hanging from one side of his mouth. I quite enjoyed that thought.

'Guy Fox is here,' I would call to Robin if she were near.

She paid no heed.

She loved the doves.

At weekends she would go into the aviary with Martyn and if I looked out one of the top windows I could see her walking from one side of the cage to the other, weighted down, it seemed to me, with white birds.

Martyn would stand and laugh as the birds hovered over her and then landed on her outstretched hands, on her shoulders, sometimes even on her head where they would burrow with their beaks in her shining hair.

I would feel sick, feeling on my own skin the scraping of their claws and the soft flicker of feathers. I would move away from the window.

I would sing to myself.

Hold my hand, I'm a stranger in Paradise.

I would turn on the radio and dance.

Slow, slow, quick, quick, slow, swooping and curving through the doors and round the furniture.

Busby Berkeley up and down the stairs, Fred Astaire on the kitchen tiles.

Later in the morning Dr Rhodes and Peter Magill would arrive, parking their car about a hundred yards down the road near the pub, I could never understand why. They almost always carried packages and they walked with care around the side of the house and across the grass. They never acknowledged my presence with more than a nod or a cool smile.

Robin would then be put out of the aviary and she would stand for a while and watch through the mesh as certain birds were cajoled into the barn and the door would be closed, then she would march over to the house, her fists clenched with rage.

'They never let me.'

'No.'

'They say it's private. What's private?'

'You know what private is. When you go into your room and shut the door, that's private.'

'That's me, alone.'

'Well this is Daddy and his friends, alone.'

'I call him Martyn.'

'That's OK.'

'I call you Star. My friends think that's a silly name.'

'I prefer Stella myself. Stella means Star, you know that, don't you?'

'Martyn told me. Martyn tells me everything.'

I laughed.

'They are magic men.'

'Who?'

'Those two private friends of Martyn's. Martyn says they're magic.'

'Sometimes Martyn tells jokes.'

'Not to me. What he tells me is real.'

'Sometimes you should take what he says with a pinch of salt.'

'What's a pinch of salt?'

He never invited me to see the inside of the barn. It was like that secret room in the flat, only more private. I could hear no sounds from it, no voices, no rustling of wings, no quiet laughter. I never had the energy to spy, peer through cracks or keyholes or run out in the evenings when the big door was open to watch the birds being brought in to roost, or on days when the side doors were open and the barn was being swept and hosed down by the boy, I never ran out to look.

Indifference, perhaps.

Was that what he felt from me?

Maybe I should have loved those birds.

Maybe I should have loved his unknown secrets.

Such thoughts never entered my head.

* * *

Some days pass quite ignominiously. Nothing stirs you, no thoughts ignite in your mind.

Looking back from here, my kitchen in Dublin, it seems to me that more than ten years of my life were ignominious.

Only a fox stirred me.

I'm not complaining.

God, how I hate people who complain; people who say if only; people who dispense blame. A stone has been thrown into the pool of my mind and I am trying to see through the ripples and the tormented reflections into the darkness below.

Robin comes into the room dressed, ready

141

for the day, as my mother might say, booted and spurred.

'Do you just hang about all day? I never understand how writers work. Do you sort of sit and wait?'

I laugh.

'For a train that may never come. Cup of coffee?'

She shakes her head.

'You drink too much coffee. Think of what it must be doing to your nervous system.'

'Nice coat.'

'Harvey Nichols. Six hundred quid.'

'Good heavens!'

'I earn it, Star. I earn...'

'Stella.'

'... a lot of money. I need a lot of money to do all the things I want to do and go to the places I want to go. I like to travel first class in aeroplanes. Martyn taught me how important it was to have money. To have a shining life, he said to me once, you have to know how to make money, and how to spend money and then make more money.'

'Did he have a shining life?' I ask this in puzzlement as it wouldn't have been an adjective that I would have attached to his life. Then I remember all those shining gifts he used to bring me, those magic offerings of love, glittering beads, bright flowers, gems, baubles.

'Yes,' I answer myself. 'Perhaps he had. I suppose it depends what you mean by shining.'

142

'For heaven's sake, Star. You're always fiddling round with words. A word is a word. A number is a number. Add a string of words together and you get a message from someone. Like sums. Two and two is four. Shining is shining.'

'It's not so simple. If only it were. Then maybe no one would write books because no one would want or need to read them.'

'Martyn once said about you that you never received his words in the spirit in which he spoke them.'

I laugh.

She frowns as she watches me laugh.

'Paranoid, he said.'

'Rubbish. Now there's a no nonsense sort of a word.'

'I'm going to walk along the sea front and then go up to Granny. I think I'll go back home this evening.'

'You do whatever you want, darling. It would be lovely if you could stay a while, but ...'

She walks towards the door.

Is she listening to me?

'... but ...'

Her hand is on the doorknob.

'I ought to get back to work. There's not much point in sitting round feeling sorry for myself. Work. I think. Yes.'

She pulls the door open.

'Do you remember the fox?'

She stands for a moment in the doorway, her back to me, her head bent slightly.

'No. I can't say I do.'

She leaves the room closing the door quietly behind her.

* * *

It was a clear morning. A huge sky and white clouds like puffs of cannon smoke. The sun was rising high, but not quite yet at its zenith.

I couldn't put a date on the day, but it was not long after Robin had started school; real school, not just the place where she went most mornings to paint and make Plasticine animals and wrote 'R is for Robin' in large meandering letters.

The fields around the house were golden and shaved and I could hear the distant rattle of a combine harvester.

I took a chip basket over my arm and went to look for blackberries. Past the aviary and the barn and the hard stubble fields behind the village. Nothing was out of place, even the clouds moved at an orderly pace. I felt quite uneasy to be living on the rim of such seductive peace.

I walked through the fields until I came to the little wood. I climbed across the ditch and began to browse through the hedgerow for berries.

A sound made me turn. In a little clearing

four fox cubs were wrestling with each other, rolling, pouncing, cuffing, gnawing. I must have been upwind of them, because they never noticed that I was there, nor did the fox, stretched beside them, asleep in the sun.

I watched them for a while, enjoying their pleasure and then crept away. It was time to fetch Robin from school.

I left my basket at the edge of the ditch and ran down the hill towards the village.

The children were milling in the school yard, making the agreeable noise of children released from rules and silence.

Robin was standing near the gate on her own.

'Why are you late?'

I took her hand.

'I'm not.'

'Yes, you are. You're always here when I come out. Where were you?'

'I have something to show you.'

'What?'

'A secret.'

'What secret?'

'Wait and see.'

'You're walking too fast.'

'No. I'm not.'

'Sta ... ar ...'

I slowed down. Her hand in mine was hot. Her hair stuck out from her head in two little bunches tied with red ribbons.

'I got a star.'

'Oh good. What for?'

'A yellow star.'

'What for, darling?'

'Yellow stars are for sums. Red stars are for writing. Blue stars are for...' She thought about blue stars...

We turned off the street up a lane towards the fields.

'Where are we going?'

'Secret.'

'My case is too heavy. I want to go home.'

I bent down and took her case from her.

'Soon. What are blue stars for?'

'Reading. Elizabeth got a blue star. Elizabeth is my best friend.'

'That's good.'

'Can I have Elizabeth to tea?'

'May I. Yes of course, darling.'

'When?'

'Whenever you like. Tomorrow, if it suits her mummy.'

'And Helen?'

'Yes.'

'And Caroline?'

'Anyone you like, darling.'

'We are all best friends. I'm tired.'

'We won't be long. Just a few more minutes and then we'll go home.'

'Caroline has a pony.'

'How lovely.'

'I'd like a pony.'

'You'll have to discuss it with Daddy.'

We came to the entrance to the wood.

'We have to be very quiet for a while. Just sssh. Not a word.'

'Why?'

I put my finger to my lips and squeezed her hand tight...

The cubs were still there, not any longer tussling with such energy, but stretching and clawing with each other and rolling over and over on the grass. The fox still lay in the same place.

We stood and watched them, Robin's hand still held tight in mine.

'Caroline has a puppy too,' she said.

The fox was on its feet at once, head up, yellow eyes staring in our direction. It turned and walked with care into the shadow of the trees, followed obediently by the cubs. I heard a slight crackling of dead twigs and they were gone.

'Baby foxes,' I said. 'Weren't they sweet?'

'Could I have one?'

'I don't think so. It wouldn't be fair really. They're wild things. They're not like cats and dogs. They don't like to live in houses.'

'Is that the secret?'

I nodded. Her face showed her disappointment. She disentangled her hand from mine.

'Was that the mummy or the daddy?'

'I'm not sure. Probably the mummy.'

'What do they eat?'

'Well ... er ... rabbits. Things like that.'

She turned away and started to walk back along the side of the ditch.

'Do they eat people?'

'Of course they don't eat people.'

'Wolves eat people. A wolf ate little Red Riding Hood's granny.'

'Foxes don't.'

'If you left a baby out in the garden. A teeny weeny baby.'

She measured the size of the baby with her hands.

'About the size of a rabbit. Would they then?'

I didn't say anything.

She nudged me with her elbow.

'Would they eat that, Star? That's what I want to know.'

'No,' I said. 'They don't eat people.'

'Not even babies?'

'Not even babies.'

We walked in silence for a while.

'I bet they do,' she said eventually. 'I bet you're just saying that. Will you ring Elizabeth's mummy when we get home and ask her to tea?'

'Yes.'

*   *   *

'I have to go and look at the sea.'

I remember saying that one Saturday

morning.

I used to miss the sea so much: that folding and unfolding, grey, green, blue, white rims of spray, the birds mewing and hovering, lofting wings outspread, the smell of salt and seaweed always in your nose. The loss sometimes became so strong that I felt unhinged with longing.

'Yuck, the sea,' said Robin landlocked, eating her cornflakes.

I was in my jeans and a sweatshirt, the keys of the car jingling in my hand.

Martyn looked up from the paper.

'I'll mind her if you're not too long.'

'Two, three hours.'

'I need the car this afternoon. Want to go with Mummy to the sea?'

'I certainly do *not*.'

It wasn't really the best day for the sea. A ragged wind blew from the north-east and on the coast there was little shelter. Flashes of white birds against the dark clouds and flashes of white waves flickered on the dark swell. The stones groaned under my feet, as they were sucked and spewed by the incoming tide. Everything was grey. My sweatshirt was the only colour. I held my arms out in front of me and was shocked by the redness; normally unremarkable, here it seemed to violate the sombreness around me.

I walked for about an hour, or rather slipped and scrambled over the stones, which sounded

149

hollow under my feet. The whole world sounded hollow, like a huge echoing cave. I kept just above the sea line and sometimes a gull would swoop and mew and soar again, the only sound that could be heard above the growling sea.

Save me...

I saw with my eyes those two words written on the wall of my scoured head.

Graffiti.

In red.

Scrawled in red looping letters.

Just those two words written in violating red.

There one moment and gone the next.

I stopped walking and watched a bird dive down into the sea.

'Not me,' I said aloud.

To whom do those words apply?

Not me.

I don't need saving.

I turned and began the walk back towards the car.

Who is writing such messages on the wall of my brain?

Who the fuck?

Why are you bothering me?

Despoiling my internal architecture?

Take your graffiti somewhere else and leave me in peace.

I don't want to be bothered.

No?

No.

He was standing at the door when I arrived back, jingling the coins in his pocket. His eyes were the colour of the stones on the beach.

I could still smell the salt coming off my clothes and hair.

'It's late.'

He held out his hand and I put the keys into it.

'It's afternoon,' I said.

'Late.'

'Oh darling.' I leant forward to kiss him, but he turned his face away and I felt foolish and guilty.

'I'm sorry, I didn't know you were going out.'

'I told you I wanted the car. That usually means one is going out, doesn't it? Doesn't it?'

I went past him into the hall.

'What time will you be back?'

'I haven't the foggiest idea.'

'You're being rather ...'

'Rather what?'

'Oh nothing. I just wondered about dinner. What time ...?'

He rattled the coins once more.

'Don't bother about dinner.'

'It's no bother. I just wondered what time ...?'

'I said, don't bother. I may spend the night in town.'

He turned and walked away towards the car.

151

There might be sand and little stones on the floor I thought, suddenly anxious.

Robin appeared from the sitting-room, eating an apple.

She looked at me for a moment or two before speaking.

'You've upset Daddy,' she said.

I closed the hall door and we both stood listening as he slammed the car door and drove off.

'We went for a walk,' she said.

'Lovely, darling. Where?'

'Secret.' She went back into the sitting-room.

*   *   *

Secrets seemed to be everywhere.

Secrets were becoming weapons.

Our areas of communication seemed to be shrinking with each new secret.

It didn't take long to find out where Robin and Martyn had walked.

The following Saturday evening he came in from the pub, his face illuminated with pleasure. I realised when I saw him that I had almost forgotten how he had been when I first met him. Dr Rhodes and Peter Magill had appeared early that morning and the three of them had spent all morning in the barn, only coming out about six o'clock in the evening. They looked so cheerful as they crossed the

152

grass that I had waved to them from the kitchen window and Dr Rhodes had inclined his head in my direction.

'I'll be back in time for dinner at eight,' Martyn had shouted towards me.

I had just finished reading a story to Robin when I heard him come in. She was tucked up, ready for sleep.

'Good-night, sleep tight, don't let the bugs bite.'

The rituals were all disposed of.

He came running up the stairs, his radiant face hurling me back into the past. I turned and followed him back into Robin's room. He switched on the light.

'Sweetheart.'

She sat up and held out her arms to him.

For a moment he flexed his fingers in the way that I recognised as part of his preparation, then he leant gently towards her and drew from under her tumbled hair a small tawny object. She looked puzzled and put out her hand to take the object.

'What is it?'

I knew.

He smiled at her.

'It's the tail of a baby fox. I met the whip in the pub and he asked me to give it to you. It's a prize.'

She took the brush from his hand and then rubbed it against her cheek.

'Nice,' she said. 'Soft. Lovely. Nice Daddy,

153

thank you. I bet Caroline doesn't have one of these.'

I left the room and ran downstairs. My head and heart were thudding with anger. I sat down at the kitchen table. I shut my eyes tight to stop tears spattering out and I saw in the darkness the ghostly yellow eyes staring at me accusingly. I heard Martyn's footsteps on the stairs. He came into the room and flicked on the light.

'Always sitting in the dark, my Star. Dinner ready?'

'Why did you do that?'

'Do what?'

'You know well. That horrible thing.'

'I didn't do anything horrible. I just told the hunt whip where the bloody things hung out. Robin showed me last Saturday.'

'But why? They were...'

'They killed my birds. Remember?'

'... only cubs. Little cubs.'

'Vermin. They went up this morning with the young hounds. Cubbing it's called.'

'I don't give a shit what it's called.'

'Training the young hounds. Blooding them. They killed my birds.'

'They didn't kill your birds. They weren't even born when your birds were killed.'

'Well, they won't get the chance to kill them in the future.' He laughed. 'I've been waiting such a long time to get my own back on the bugger.'

154

'I didn't realise you carried grudges.'

'You could call it justice. I believe in justice. An eye for an eye. Good principle.'

'The world has changed a bit since those words were written.'

'Don't believe it, Star. Don't ever believe it. What about food? I'm starving.'

'I'd rather you didn't teach Robin such lessons.'

He opened a cupboard and took out a bottle of wine.

'Lessons?'

He was looking for the corkscrew. His voice was disinterested.

'Yes. Eye-for-eye lessons.'

He picked the screwdriver out from a drawer.

'Food,' he said and left the room with the bottle and the corkscrew.

When I went into the dining-room with the dishes on a tray, he was sitting in his place, a glass of wine in his hand.

'Beautiful Star,' he said, holding up his glass towards me.

'Do you understand what I'm saying?'

'No moral lectures, please. I don't need a middle-class Irishwoman to tell me how I should behave.'

'You might do worse.'

'Not much.'

We ate our dinner in silence; we eventually went to bed in silence and when in bed he pulled me towards him, I pushed him away.

*   *   *

She has gone out to compose herself.

The wind will pull her this way and that, I can hear it racing across the bay and trembling the branches of my tree.

The spray from waves will light on her face.

Her hair will tangle and maybe when she gets to my mother's house she will break the teeth of her comb trying to order it once more.

Darkness streams in from the past.

Makes me melancholic.

Never for too long, my nature is buoyant, like one of his doves ...

I wondered when I heard the news if those doves had been the descendants of the ones I had known in the aviary.

How many generations descended?

Robin would not know the answer to that question; anyway, I suspect it would be an inappropriate question to ask.

My mother will ask her questions.

She will settle her deep in an armchair and shower her with questions.

Why?

How?

When, dear?

Who?

Will she answer or evade?

I know her so little that I can't answer that

question.

'I know what you're thinking,' my mother used to say to me and I would say, 'Tell me then if you're so clever' and she would.

At such times I would slam doors, rush out into the damp air, scream inside myself.

I loathed my own transparency.

I felt at times that she could even see the workings of my body, blood pumping, digestion doing its job, air bubbles, the heart pulsating.

She saw it all with her x-ray eyes.

*   *   *

'More than anything in the world, I want to make you happy.'

He said that not long after the episode with the fox cubs.

The child was in bed and I was lying on the sofa in the sitting-room, listening to Monteverdi. The counter-tenor and treble moved in the shadows; they built in the golden remains of the day wonderful structures of sound. Hautbois, viola da gamba, cello, the voices, all melancholic, suited the autumn evening.

I hadn't heard the car, nor his footsteps in the hall. Suddenly he was there in the room.

'*Laudate Dominum*,' the voice sang, and there was Martyn in his London suit standing just inside the door.

'More than anything in the world, I want to make you happy.'

I struggled through the clinging sounds.

Laudate Dominum.

Into the present.

He switched on the light.

'Why do you sit in the dark? How many times have I asked you that question?'

I sat up and blinked at him.

I must have looked bizarre, my head sodden with hautbois and counter-tenor. My blinking eyes suddenly filled with electricity.

Laudate Dominum.

'I want to know you. I don't know you.'

He bent down and took my hand in his.

He raised it to his lips and kissed it.

'You only need to love me.'

'I want to know you too.'

'Such greed.'

He murmured the words into the palm of my hand.

'It doesn't seem greedy to me.'

'I give you everything, don't I?'

'Yes.'

'The child. This house. My love.'

'Yes. Yes. Yes.'

'The machine to play this dismal music. Accept what I give you and...'

'*Laudate Dominum,*' I said.

His lips buried themselves in the bend of my arm, the warm crook of my elbow.

No one visited me, so when I heard the doorbell ring I was surprised to say the least of it.

When I say no one visited me, I mean, of course, through the front door. Neighbours came from time to time in through the kitchen, to have a cup of coffee, look for a child, borrow something, they also left through the kitchen door. Messages arrived in the same way. Only the postman used the front door in any formal way.

To my surprise, Bill Freeman stood outside glaring at me over a huge cardboard box.

'God, I hate the country.'

I stood, my mouth hanging open in surprise. He pushed past me and dumped the box on the hall floor. He turned and held his arms out to me.

'Bill!'

We hugged, great crushing bear hugs.

'What on earth are you doing here?'

'Visiting you, sport.'

I laughed.

'Seeing as how you never came to visit me, I thought sod her ... Coffee, darling. I have to have coffee or die ... I'll go and visit her. Make her feel guilty. So, I took the day off work. God, what a posh house!'

He picked up the box and we went into the kitchen.

159

'It took me hours to find the place. Round and round those little winding roads. I thought I might never make it. Be found dead in a ditch somewhere, dead of boredom.'

He put the box on the table and began, like Father Christmas, to take parcels out of it.

'I didn't know if there were any shops, sport, so I brought lunch for us and...'

He put a bottle of champagne on the table by the parcels.

'Why don't you speak?'

'I am overcome, overjoyed too.'

He took up my hand and kissed it.

'You look great. Countrified.'

'What does that mean?'

'But definitely great. Calm, darling. The tizzy factor smoothed out. No angst. Oh God I pray daily for no more angst.'

'Come and live in the country.'

'Not on your nell, sport. Coffee.'

I turned on the tap and water rattled into the kettle.

'Do you miss London?'

'Should I?'

'The centre of the universe.'

'Sez who?'

'Sez I. Sez the whole world's press. The whole world flocks in to clutter up the streets, breathe smog and stare. They stare at us, imagine, the legitimate Londoners. You don't know what you're missing. Soho's becoming intolerable. I may have to shift the old centre of

160

gravity. If you don't miss London, do you miss me, Missis whatever your name is?'

'I have to say yes, don't I? Seeing as how you're sitting in my kitchen waiting for me to make you coffee.'

'Or champagne. Champagne for elevenses is a fine tonic.'

He began the ritual of unwrapping, unwiring and uncorking and I got two glasses.

Pop and foam. I caught the foam in a glass.

'Isn't it sexy. Don't you get bad thoughts just seeing it foaming out like that?'

'I do hope some of the neighbours come in and get their eyes on this.'

We clinked glasses. We smiled old friendship at each other.

'Now, tell me what you're doing here.'

'I couldn't keep away from you, sport.'

'You managed very well for seven years.'

'My! Is it as long as that? I kept thinking you'd come back. Each time the door opened, I thought, this is she, that woman. She has come back at last.'

'How charming.'

'I am charming. Don't you remember?'

'It's a bit like a dream. I remember so well all that time before I got myself to London. I remember more or less everything that has happened since, but that couple of years is like a forgotten dream.'

'Even me?'

'Even you.'

'More champagne. I brought two bottles, just in case.'

He poured.

'I mustn't get drunk.'

'Why ever not?'

'I have a child I have to soberly fetch from school.'

'Split infinitive. Even in the country we have to keep the standards up. I heard about the child. Brown bread, smoked salmon, prosciutto crudo. I'm starving after that drive. Let's munch as we drink. You will then keep sober and I won't faint from hunger.'

He began to unwrap the parcels. There was also a tarte aux mirabelles.

'Boy or girl?'

'Girl.'

'Oh goody. I've never fancied little boys. How's the conjuror?'

'Fine.'

'Hmmm. You tired of him yet?'

'Shut up.'

'Whatsisname?'

'Martyn.'

'Ah yes. Mind if I smoke?'

'Go ahead.'

He took a cigar from his pocket and began to work on it.

'He's not a conjuror.'

'A tricky dick. Something like that. Come back, sport.'

'Back?' I didn't know what he meant.

162

'Yep. Back to the office. Back to the centre of the world. Life might pass you by.'

'You've come all the way down here to say that?'

'Just one of the things I came to say. You've been in my mind a lot, sport ... all jokes apart, from here on down I'm dead serious. I want you to do something for me.'

'Are you married?'

He blew a vast cloud of smoke from his mouth and laughed.

'What's so funny?'

'I thought you knew.'

I shook my head.

'You forget. Life is passing me by.'

'I'm not that way inclined. I thought you knew. I thought everyone knew. I haven't tried to hide it.'

I felt myself blushing.

'I'm sorry ...'

'No need for sorrow.'

'I didn't mean that.'

He leant across the table and took hold of my hand.

'I know what you meant.'

He pressed my knuckles with his thumb.

'I'm obviously not very good at discovering things about people.'

'Like whatsisname?'

'Even my own child. I find her alarmingly enigmatic.'

'Beat her.'

163

I laughed.

'You are a clown.'

'Children should not be allowed to puzzle their parents. Let's finish this.' He emptied the bottle into our glasses. 'Beat whatsisname too. Come back to work. Step out of this box.'

'I like this box.'

'Look, come up to London, just for one day. Come into the office. We'll have lunch, not Soho, I promise you, somewhere fearfully saloooobrious. I'd like you to meet Peter. My … I'd like you to meet Peter. Jesus Christ, I'm such a lazy sod not to have come down before, rung you, kept in touch. I was so sure…'

'Sure?'

'… you'd be back. Certain. That shows how little I know too, doesn't it, sport?'

'I'm happy here.'

'I think we had this conversation ages ago. What's happy. A cat sitting in the sun is happy.'

'I'm a cat sitting in the sun.'

'One day.'

I shook my head.

'Why not?'

I wondered why not.

'I think I'm frightened.'

'Yes. Yes.'

'I don't want to upset things, the equilibrium of my life. Martyn. It's quite a fine line I tread. Leave me be. I'm OK.'

He squeezed some lemon onto a slice of

164

smoked salmon, rolled it up and popped it into his mouth.

'I love him. That's what I was going to say when I asked you about marriage. Love … love…'

'That's OK, sport. You don't have to explain things. I understand what you're trying to say. Let's go and look at your lovely garden.'

He held my hand as we walked through the shrubs, his thumb pressing hard on my knuckles.

'And what have we here?'

'The aviary. Martyn's doves.'

He put an arm round me and hugged me tight.

The doves paid no attention to us.

'Do you eat them?'

I burst out laughing.

'Don't be silly, of course we don't eat them.'

'I believe dove is very tender. Corn-fed doves. They eat them somewhere. Italy probably.'

'Not Suffolk.'

'Why doves, then? Why not budgerigars, parakeets, humming birds, something exotic and colourful? Mandarin ducks? Quaack. Why doves?'

'I don't know. He doesn't tell me. I think he's training them.'

'Training them? God, you're such an ass, Stella. Why don't you ask him?'

'I can't.'

165

'Why ever not?'

'Because he won't tell me and then I will feel humiliated. I've learnt not to ask him questions. If he wants me to know something, he'll tell me. That's the way we lead our lives. That seems fair enough.'

He must have felt my embarrassment, because he clapped his hands, suddenly, together.

The birds, alarmed, flew up and hovered anxiously near the top of the cage.

'Don't,' I said. 'Leave them alone. Leave them their tranquillity.'

He tapped with a finger on the wire, creating a ripple of sound that in turn created a ripple of wings above us.

'Like you?'

'Yes.' I turned and walked away from him.

I wanted to cry.

I wanted him to go back to London.

I could hear him following me across the grass.

'You see, sport, the fact that you're angry with me ...'

'I'm not angry with you.'

'... means ...'

I stopped walking and waited until he caught up with me.

'I don't want you to tell me what it means. I don't want your potted psychology. I want gossip. Tell me gossip, funny stories. Who's shagging who, all that sort of thing. You used

to tell such great stories. Tell me about Peter ...
About you and Peter. Just don't tell me about
me, because you know nothing.'

He put out a hand and touched my face.

'Right on, sport. I always thought, if I hadn't
been the way I am, I would like to have married
you. There is something in your being that
appeals greatly to me. Let's go in, finish the
food, have that coffee and I'll show you the
present I brought you.'

He leant down and kissed my cheek.

'I'm sorry. Always forgive. I remain your
humble servant, yours sincerely, Bill.'

I laughed. He gave me a gentle shove
towards the house.

Yellow and orange leaves fluttered on the
grass as a little wind whipped round the corner
of the house.

In the kitchen he pointed towards the box on
the table.

'Prezzy, sport. All that country air has made
me starving and thirsty. Open it up and I'll pop
another cork.'

He produced another bottle from a large
paper bag.

I looked into the box with caution.

There was a portable typewriter in a neat
black leather case and two reams of A4.

Pop.

The leather was soft and expensive.

I unzipped the case and looked at the
keyboard.

167

He put a foaming glass down beside me.

'I know it's a crappy gesture out of a sentimental novel, but I'd like you to take on board the intention behind it.'

'It looks very expensive.'

'It is. Italian chic. I look on it as an investment. Given time, words will flow easily onto the keys.'

He buttered some brown bread.

'God, I love food. By the time I'm sixty, I'll probably weigh sixteen stone. Have some prosciutto. Let me butter you a slice of bread. Squeeze of lemon? Say something, for heaven's sake.'

'Yes.'

He took that as some all-embracing affirmative and smiled.

He handed me something that I couldn't possibly fit into my mouth.

'There you are then. Future all mapped out. I feel like St George. Fine day. One damsel saved. Now I can go back to London triumphant. God save the queen. You notice I used a lower case q.'

'I can't type.'

'Try. It's dead easy. Qwertyuiop. So they say.'

He raised his glass in my direction.

'Qwertyuiop.'

I laughed and raised my glass in return.

'Qwertyuiop.'

I ran my fingers over the top row of keys.

The little hammers rose and fell, pattering gently, like hailstones on a window.

'I love it.'

'Phew!'

He sat down at the table and reached for some more prosciutto.

'You can write me a thank you letter on it and then turn your hand to matters more important. Now, eat. I can guarantee that the tarte aux mirabelles will be sublime.'

* * *

It was.

I remember now as I sit at my table with my back to the window, the sweet astringency of that tarte aux mirabelles. I remember the thick yellow Jersey cream, that you couldn't buy now even if you wanted to.

My mother might find some, somewhere or other.

She has always believed in a good, balanced diet, which would include, in moderation, of course, thick, yellow Jersey cream.

He believed that hidden inside me was a writer.

I never knew how he discovered that before I did myself. Maybe I would never have allowed myself to discover it, if it hadn't been for Bill.

I wish I still had the typewriter. The black leather case would be somewhat the worse for the wear, but the hammers might still rise and

169

fall with the ease they did on the day we ate the Jersey cream.

Bill is dead.

His death is irrelevant to this story, but I have to write it down.

I hate to write it down.

This is the first time I have written it down.

I hate those three words.

I have to write those three words.

Bill.

Is.

Dead.

He didn't even die as exotically as Martyn, in a shower of feathers.

Fast.

Martyn was here one minute and gone the next.

Fast.

My fingers will not stop now on the qwertyuiop until they have had their little say.

This is not Bill's story. I say that to them, but they stutter on.

Six months ago I sat beside him and Peter too, who is not yet dead, but may be soon, such is the viciousness of love.

I sat on his right side.

I held his right hand in my hand and the sun shone across my shoulder onto the foot of the bed. The bedcover was blue and it weighted on his tiny body, crushing him into the softness of the mattress.

So much for weighing sixteen stone, sport, I

thought.

There was almost nothing left of him.

Spirit and pain really, that was all.

Peter held his left hand gently between his two hands.

I don't think he had slept for days and his face was pale, his fingers trembled.

My fingers trembled.

Bill's breath trembled in his throat.

There was so little of him left for us to love now, only the trembling breath and his cold hands.

I bent down and kissed his hand.

I felt as if my lips were burning a hole in his cold flesh.

'Dear sport,' I said.

Peter laughed gently.

'I hope he can hear you.'

'I'm sure he can.'

Peter bent down and as I had done kissed the hand that lay between his.

'Go to God, sport.'

Bill sighed.

It sounded like a sigh.

It was, in reality, death.

*   *   *

'I don't believe in God.'

I said that to my mother, three or four days after Bill's funeral.

I was sitting in her drawing-room drinking

171

tea and the spring sun was shining across my shoulder as it had done at the moment of Bill's death.

My mother stirred her tea and said nothing.

'Do you?' I asked.

'Of course, dear. And in the resurrection of the body and the life of the world to come.'

'How lucky you are.'

'You have the option.'

'I suppose so.'

She smiled for a moment.

'I don't suppose it matters very much whether you do or not. He sees into your heart. He understands. I'm sure your friend Bill is in His good hands.'

'Thank you,' I said.

*   *   *

After Bill had left the house and before I went, somewhat tipsily, to collect Robin from school, I carried the typewriter upstairs and put it in the back of my wardrobe, behind a pile of shoes, well hidden from the eyes of magicians and small inquisitive children.

I was in the kitchen when Martyn came home.

He came straight across the hall and stood in the kitchen doorway.

'Who's been here?'

His nose had caught the smell of cigar smoke.

172

'Bill. You remember Bill?'

'Bill?'

'My boss. Yes ... In the days when I worked. Bill.'

Robin came bumping down the stairs on her bottom.

'Daddy, Daddy, Daddy.'

'Oh, him. What on earth brought him here?'

'He came to see me.'

'Daddy.'

'After all this time?'

'After all this time.'

'Hello, Daddy.'

He put his arms round her and lifted her off the ground.

'Hello, my little bird.'

'Mummy had champagne.'

'Lucky Mummy.'

'Can I come and feed the doves with you?'

'May I, and it's past your bedtime,' I said.

'Of course you can. I'd be glad of your company.'

He took her hand and they walked together out of the back door.

I watched them as they crossed the grass, still hand in hand. It was starting to get dark and the doves were murmuring. Robin said something to Martyn and I heard his laugh floating in the air.

I suddenly felt very lonely.

*   *   *

QWERTYUIOP. I wrote the letters on a postcard and went down to the village and bought a stamp.

Mrs Brown pushed the stamp under the brass bars without a word, without a smile, and I pushed twopence halfpenny back at her.

'Thank you,' I said.

'Your husband want to sell some of them birds?'

'I don't know. I shouldn't think so, but I'll ask him if you like.'

'I think they're pretty. I wouldn't mind having a couple of them walking round my garden. I said that to my Alec and he said ask. There's no harm in asking.'

'They might eat your vegetables.'

'We don't grow vegetables. We buy vegetables. He ain't one for hard work. Digging and that. What's wrong with buying vegetables anyway? I thought a couple of birds would be nice. Cooing out the back.'

'I'll ask him. I'll let you know.'

She closed down her face again and I went out and dropped the postcard into the letterbox.

Those were the first letters that I had written on the machine.

Big bloody deal.

Probably the last.

I heard the postcard slithering into the darkness.

I'm not a writer.

I don't know what to write about.

For three weeks I had ignored the thing; left it to moulder behind my shoes, hoping beyond hope that it would disappear and I would no longer be bothered by its presence in my life.

Someone else's expectations, not mine, I said to myself several times a day.

Shut up, I would shout up the stairs towards it, from time to time. Don't be annoying me. Get lost.

Then I took it out one day and wrote QWERTYUIOP on a postcard.

After that I rolled some paper in and wrote ASDFGHJKL.

Then, ZXCVBNM.

The sound of the keys pattering on the paper suddenly became the most seductive sound that I had ever heard.

I wrote ... I don't want this.

I wrote ... How do you teach yourself to write?

I wrote ... When do you know if you can or not?

Once upon a time.

What is the next word to be?

What will happen in my life when I discover that word?

What is there to be afraid of?

An object in a soft leather case, hidden behind a pile of shoes.

*   *   *

175

One of the doves escaped one day.

I don't know how.

It must have flown out when the boy who cleaned the aviary was inside.

The leaves had been drifting off the trees for a long time, and I had moved from once upon a time to a story about a woman trapped in a room with a bird, torn between her terror of the fluttering creature and her guilt at being unable to help it in its terror. She was going to leave it to die, battering its tiny body against the solidity of the window. I lifted my eyes from the keys and looked out of the window, searching for words and there, on an almost bare branch, sat a white dove.

'Oh shit,' I said aloud.

I used to keep the rooms warm with my own words, when no one else was in the house.

The bird seemed to have no desire to fly away. It looked as if it were waiting for something to happen, its head hunched slightly to one side.

I went downstairs and out into the garden. I could see the flash of white among the remaining orange leaves.

I went over to the aviary fence, calling the boy's name as I went.

'Johnny.'

There was no one there and the door of the barn was locked.

Johnny had gone home.

'If I were you, bird,' I called up to it, 'I'd get

the hell out while you can. Living in a cage is strictly for the birds.'

I laughed a loud, corny laugh.

The bird launched itself off the branch and began to flap its way down towards me.

I ran into the house and shut the door.

I made sure all the windows were shut and I went back to my typewriter and thought about fear and freedom and listened to the pattering of the keys until it was time to go and collect Robin from school.

'One of Daddy's birds got out,' I said to her as we walked along the road towards home.

She twisted her head round and looked up at me.

'Which one?'

'How on earth would I know which one? They all look the same to me.'

'He knows them all.'

'I didn't realise.'

'He'll be cross.'

'Probably. I tried to find Johnny, but he'd gone.'

'Johnny couldn't do a thing. Martyn says he's hopeless. He can wield a hose. That's what Martyn says.'

There was a long silence. Our feet crunched on the pebbly surface of the road.

'What's wield?'

I told her.

Back at the house she threw her satchel on the floor in the hall and went out into the garden. I followed her.

The dove had flown back to the top of the tree again and sat, its feathers ruffled against the wind.

Robin looked up at the bird for a moment or two.

'Easy peasy,' she said.

'You're not going to climb up there after it, in case that is what is in your head.'

She didn't even bother to react to that.

She ran back into the house and I waited in the garden and wondered what had happened to me in my childhood days to make me so frightened of birds. Nothing sprang to mind.

My mother had had an old aunt with a parrot. I remembered that. If you put your finger in through the bars of its cage, it would bite you. I remembered that too.

'Just don't put your finger in its cage,' my mother had said. 'Then there's nothing to be afraid of. Anyway, it's probably got some terrible African disease. Avoid it.'

I avoided it.

'There,' said Robin, pushing a key into my hand.

'What's this?'

'The key of the barn. Martyn always keeps it in the pocket of his brown coat.'

She gave me a push towards the barn.

'Inside the door there's a big bin full of corn...'

'I can't go into the barn...'

'Oh Mummy, don't be so silly. It's too high up for me to reach into. You'll have to go. Bring me back a handful, then the silly thing will come down. You'll see. Easy peasy.'

I felt rather like Bluebeard's wife as I turned the key in the door. Inside it was high and quite cold. I could hear the birds rustling and cooing from the aviary. The bin was black and ran almost the whole length of the wall. I opened the lid and leaning in scooped up a handful of corn and then carefully closed the lid down again. At the far end of the barn was a high platform and along the wall on each side, high scaffolds held banks of lights.

Out in the garden Robin was waiting for me, her hands outstretched. Carefully I poured the corn from my hand into the cup of her fists.

'Go in now, and don't come out, whatever you do. I'm in charge. You have to do what I say.'

I went in and closed the kitchen door and watched out of the window as she stood in the middle of the grass, her hands held up towards the bird. She was quite still. Only the wind caught at her hair and teased and pulled it around her head. After about five minutes I heard a flapping in the tree and the bird flew down, hovering for a while above her before landing on her wrist and beginning to peck delicately at the corn in the hollow of her hands. With great care she moved her free hand and gently placed it on the bird's back.

The bird continued to eat as she walked across the garden and into the barn. It didn't seem to mind being captured.

Robin was in the bath when Martyn came home.

I was scrubbing her neck with a soapy flannel, she hated that.

'Ow. You always hurt. I can do it myself.'

'You can't. You just pat at it. You leave the grime.'

'Ow, ow, ow.'

Then we heard the door.

'Martyn,' she said to me. 'Daddy,' she shouted in welcome. 'I saved one of your birds today. How about that?'

He came running up the stairs and into the bathroom.

'How about what, precious?'

He bent down to kiss her slippery, steaming body.

He held out a hand to me and as I took it, I felt the liquidity of silk slipping through my fingers. A long, brilliantly coloured scarf poured from my hand down onto the floor.

'Darling, how beautiful.'

'Me, me, me,' splashed Robin.

'Out first, little bird, and let Mummy dry you.'

'No, you. You dry me. Mummy hurts.'

She scrambled to her feet.

'Mummy rubs too hard. Mummy scratches the skin off my bones.'

He laughed.

'Such nonsense. No more nonsense. Out you get. Wetness spoils the magic.'

She jumped out of the bath and I wrapped a towel round her.

'Like electricity?' she asked.

I blotted and rubbed and pummelled.

'Like electricity,' he agreed.

I pulled her nightdress over her head and she wriggled away from me. She stood beside him, waiting.

He held his hands out towards her, palms down towards the floor.

'Have you been very good?'

'Yes.'

I leant down and pulled the plug out of the bath. The water began to swirl and gurgle.

'Mummy's not paying attention.'

'Mummystar. Watch him.'

'I'm watching.'

For a moment he turned his hands palms up so that we could see their emptiness and then down again.

Different colours of smoke began to drift up through his fingers, pale blue and pink and a sulphurous yellow. Straight up the little pillars rose into the steamy air. Her eyes followed their rise. He put his fingertips together as if he were praying and little stars sparked from his fingertips.

'Daddy.'

He opened his hands out into a bowl which

was filled with chocolates, each one wrapped in gold or silver paper. He tumbled them into her outstretched hands.

'Oooh, Daddy.'

The threads of smoke melted into the steam, leaving behind just the faintest whiff of sulphur.

'Magic.'

'What about saying thank you,' I said somewhat boringly.

She began to unwrap one of the chocolates.

'You'll have to wash your teeth again.'

'I saved one of your birds today.'

'You did?'

He looked surprised.

'How was that? What happened?'

'One of them got out and Mummy didn't know what to do, so I got it back in the cage when I came home from school.'

'What a clever girl you are.'

He looked at me. His eyes were starting their slide into grey.

I squeezed out Robin's flannel and hung it on the side of the bath.

'How did it happen? How did one of the birds get out? Have there been more bloody foxes around the place?'

'No. Nothing like that. I think Johnny must have let it out by mistake. It flew up into the chestnut tree. It was all right. It just sat up there, waiting to be rescued. Luckily...'

'Are you sure there isn't a hole in the

netting?'

'I don't think so.'

'Did you look?'

I shook my head.

'Why didn't you look? Any number of them could have escaped.'

'I'm sorry. It didn't occur to me. Everything is all right. The bird is back in. No harm is done.'

'If you weren't so foolish about birds we wouldn't have to have that fool Johnny around the place. I'll go and check the netting.'

As he turned to leave the room, Robin spoke again.

'Mummy has a typewriter.'

I remembered that I had forgotten to put it away when I went to collect her from school.

He stopped in his tracks.

'A what?'

'A typewriter. In her room. I saw it when I went to get the key of the barn. Can I use it?'

'Where did you get a typewriter?'

'I...'

'Well?'

I felt the heat rushing up, covering my neck and face.

'Bill gave it to me...'

'Bill? All those weeks ago and you never said. What is all this?'

'It's nothing. It's just a typewriter. I couldn't make my mind up whether to send it back to him or not. I ... He ... He gave it to me. A

183

surprise present. Unsolicited gift.'

'Truth, Star.'

Robin stood between us turning her head from one of us to the other as if she were watching a tennis match. As she watched she chewed chocolate.

'What do you mean, truth? Why shouldn't I have a typewriter? It's not a lethal weapon.'

'I want to know why that pouf came all the way down here to give you ... I want to know why you didn't tell me. I want to know what you think you're at?'

'I'm at nothing. He gave it to me as a present. He wants me to write a novel ... well something. That's all. He thinks I should try. He ...'

He was laughing.

'You?'

'What's so funny?'

'A writer? What do you have to write about? For God's sake, haven't you enough to do without fiddling around with a typewriter? Who does that fellow think you are, Ernest Hemingway? Pardon me if I laugh.'

'No. I won't. Come on Robin, wash your teeth and then into bed. We'll put the rest of the chocolates away until tomorrow.'

He went out of the room, still laughing, and ran down the stairs.

I squeezed toothpaste onto her brush and handed it to her.

My eyes were dizzy with tears.

I heard the kitchen door slam.

Robin spat chocolate and toothpaste into the basin.

'Rinse,' I said.

She rinsed.

'Why wouldn't you pardon him if he laughed?' she asked.

*   *   *

I wore the long red silk scarf as we sat having dinner in the kitchen.

We ate in silence.

After he had come in from inspecting the aviary he had poured himself a drink and gone into the sitting-room.

He had come when I called him for dinner but he hadn't spoken.

'Next Saturday, Rhodes and Magill and a couple of others will be here for lunch. About fifteen, I'd say.'

He was eating a pear and the juice ran down over his chin.

'Yes. Fifteen.'

He mopped at his chin with his napkin.

'This coming Saturday.'

'As I said. I presume there isn't a problem.'

'Of course not. I just...'

'Something substantial. Nothing arty farty. Good solid food. We've got something to show them at last.'

185

He leant towards me, eyes alive and sparking again.

'Something fabulous.'

'That's wonderful, darling. I . . .'

'Rhodes and Magill will be staying in the hotel for the rest of the week and we'll just be perfecting the show. Putting the last touches. Making it really crisp. Professional. I will leave all the front of house stuff to you. Feed them. Charm them. Put them in a good mood. Right?'

'I'll do my best. Who are they?'

He gestured impatiently with his hands.

'People. That's all, people.'

He got up from the table.

'I won't have any coffee. I'm just going down to the hotel for an hour or so. See they've settled in all right. Don't wait up for me. We'll have the typewriter conversation when all this is over.'

*   *   *

I still have dreams, or perhaps they are more like nightmares, about that afternoon.

The sound of wings beating over our heads in the darkness, like some frightening second coming.

My hands were clenched together, slippery with fear.

Martyn's face, white in the spotlight, high above as if hanging in the air.

The rippling of wings as the light caught them, white waves stirring in the darkness.

No command.

No order given, but the gleaming angel appears above us flying, silver face, body feathered from top to toe and the great beating wings outstretched ... Just the sound of wings and the breathing of the man sitting beside me.

Then slowly to the right, the glimmering of another shadowy figure, more wings, and another and yet another and soon the whole space was filled with flying falling angels. We could hear them rushing through the air and then suddenly there was darkness so total that we were all shocked and through the darkness the sound of long sighs and what seemed to be the sussurations of silk skirts rustling in the breeze. Then the lights came up and we sat and blinked at each other. We looked foolish, blinking in the barn, with the scaffolds and the angled lights, ticking now as they cooled down, and the empty stage.

Suddenly there was a frantic flapping of wings and out from behind one of the lamp brackets flew a solitary dove. It circled the roof, looking for a way out and finding none, it swooped down towards us.

I pushed past the man beside me and made for the door.

Outside it was brilliant sun and the birds were settling to their perches; just a few feathers drifted on the air.

The last to leave were Dr Rhodes and Peter Magill.

'I think that went well,' were the only words Dr Rhodes spoke to me. 'Mrs ... ah ... Glover.'

I smiled at him.

'Wonderful.'

Peter Magill didn't speak, he just inclined his head and lifted one finger as he passed me.

'Goodbye, Mr Magill,' I called after him, but he didn't seem to hear.

The both got into their car and went away.

'Where do they go?' I asked Martyn who was standing just behind me. 'Do they have wives and families or what?'

'Of course they do. At least Peter has a wife and a dog.'

'How great for him.'

'He is a genius.'

'Really?'

'He can do anything in the world with lights and as you can imagine lights are a major factor ... He has a highly advanced imagination and great technical skill.'

I closed the hall door and we stood side by side in the hall. I think we both felt that anticlimactic feeling that always comes after some high point has been achieved. Tristesse.

'Well?' His voice was anxious.

'It was amazing. Astonishing. Triumphant.'

I put my arms around his neck and kissed him.

'Powerful.'

He said nothing, just stood there in my embrace. He needed me to say the right word, make the right gesture before he would speak.

'I never realised that you were working on something as spectacular as that.'

He moved away from me, a small smile on his face.

'Spectacular,' he said. 'Yes.'

'What happens now?'

He began to dance around the hall, beating with his fists at the air.

'The world. We'll bring it round the world. Our show. Our bloody brilliant show. This is just a beginning. We've much further to go with this one and then there will be more. I can see thousands of birds, not just hundreds. Thousands. This is just a tiny beginning. Just you wait and see. World...'

He sank down onto the bottom step of the stairs, put his head in his hands and began to cry.

I went across the hall and put my hand on his head.

'Darling...'

He shook my hand away.

'You hated it. Speak the truth.'

'I didn't, darling. I thought it was wonderful. I thought it was all those things I said.'

'I know the way you feel. There's no point in telling me lies.'

'You're tired. You're overwrought.'

I sounded like my mother.

'It's been a wonderful day. A triumph. Come on, you need to relax. Come and sit down and have a drink.'

'If you don't like it, I'll stop the whole thing now. There's no need to go one step further. I can give it all up. Now. Tomorrow.'

'I love it, I tell you. I wouldn't want you to give it up. I really want you to go on and on and on.'

His eyes gleamed through his fingers.

'True?'

'Have I ever told you lies?'

'You've kept secrets from me.'

'That's not lies. Everyone has mad thoughts in their heads that belong just to them. I think your act was great. Now, come and have a drink...'

I looked up and saw Robin standing on the landing staring down at us.

'You should be asleep,' I said.

'I want Daddy to come and tuck me up.'

'Daddy's tired.'

He jumped to his feet.

'Of course I will.'

'And tell me a story.'

'Mummy's the story-teller around here. I'll tuck you in and hold your hand for a few minutes.'

He started up the stairs.

*   *   *

Some man rang up once and on hearing that Martyn wasn't at home said, 'Is that Angela?' When I said no, he rang off immediately.

I told Martyn after dinner that night. He didn't say anything for a long time. He looked past me at the door of a cupboard, as if he were looking at words printed on it.

He frowned.

He pursed his lips together.

'Who is Angela, anyway?' he said at last.

'I presume she's your secretary.'

'Angela hasn't been my secretary for years. You know that.'

'No, I don't. You never told me. What happened to her?'

'She left. I told you. I remember telling you. She got a better job. Got married too, I think. Yes. She got married. Haven't seen her for years.'

Lies, I thought, looking at his face.

'What's your present secretary's name?'

'Peggy.'

'Any good?'

'She's OK. Why do you ask?'

'Interest. I am interested in what you do, you know. Or, I would be if you'd tell me about it. Darling, we've been married for years and I know nothing about what happens to you from the moment you go out through that door until the moment you come back in. Nothing. It hurts a bit, you know. It's as if you don't trust me with your life. I hate that feeling.'

191

'Curiosity killed the cat,' was all he said.

He was away after that for long periods of time. Without warning he would go, without warning he would come back. Sometimes Peter Magill would arrive with a van and sixty or seventy birds would be caught and caged and stacked neatly on specially built shelves in the back of the van. They seemed quite comfortable to be shifted round like this and murmured in an amiable fashion as they were carried out of the aviary. Peter Magill would then drive off, followed by Martyn in his own car.

From time to time postcards would arrive for Robin from East Germany, Hungary, Poland.

You are my best bird. I miss you. Love Daddy.

Nothing ever came for me.

*   *   *

I could string two sentences together. I discovered that about myself. I was beginning to need to write. Phrases, sentences snaked from my head through my fingers and onto the page. I was learning how to order them, how to choose from this can of snakes in my head, the words that were appropriate, and to leave to one side the inappropriate. The long disused thesaurus in my mind slowly began to open its pages to me once more.

192

I went by bus one day to Ipswich to buy typewriter ribbons and several boxes of A4 at W. H. Smith.

'Writing a novel?' asked the girl at the cash desk.

'I think so.'

She looked impressed.

'Should I know your name?'

'Not yet.'

Such folly makes me laugh.

* * *

'Where do you go?'

We lay warm in bed, his arms curled round me, the smell of our bodies a comfortable protection.

'You're always asking questions.'

'You never answer them. I have always been a person of insatiable curiosity.'

He pulled his arms from round my body and sat up. I put a hand on his leg, but he twitched it away.

'Don't I give you everything you want? Do you and the child need for anything? Have you any complaints?'

I shook my head.

'No complaints.'

'Well then, for the last time leave me alone. Stop needing to know things about me that are none of your business. You have your secrets too. Remember that. You have your

193

typewriter. Inside your head you have secrets you won't share with me. How do you think I feel about that? You run away from me into your mind. Bloody rabbit warren. I don't want you to be in there. I want you out here. Out here where I can see you. See what is going on.'

'That's hardly reasonable.'

'What's reasonable about marriage? I give you everything you need. What do you give me?'

'I look after you. I love you. I didn't ask for this house, did I? You bought this house for yourself, not for me. Don't try to pretend it was any other way. I mind it for you. I keep it comfortable and welcoming for you to return to. All I want to know is where you go and what you're doing. Who are you, Martyn? You can tell me that while you're at it.'

He got out of bed and put on his dressing-gown. As he tied the silk cord round his waist he leant towards me. His eyes were sheets of grey.

'I thought when I got you that you'd be the perfect wife for me. That you'd get on with the job of being a wife, that you wouldn't cause trouble. I want a quiet life when I'm here. I find you are becoming intolerable. Slippy.'

'This is ridiculous.'

'It's what you have been asking for. You've been at me for years, ferreting, making judgements in your head. I've put up with all that patiently, but now you're trying to lead

194

some secondary life of your own. I won't have that and...'

'This is a dangerous conversation.'

I put my hand out towards him, but he pretended not to see it.

'Words like this lodge in your head; sometimes they're quite difficult to forget.'

'I don't want you to forget them. I want you to understand I mean what I say.'

'I'm not a performing dove.'

'No,' he said. 'You're not.'

'I love you.'

'You love yourself.'

He turned and walked away from me, across the room.

'Yes. We all do that. You do that too.'

At the door he turned and looked at me.

'You need to learn a lot.'

He went out of the room and closed the door behind him.

*   *   *

The telephone rings.

I get up and go into the hall to answer it.

I really must buy one of those cordless things that I can carry round in my pocket and use in all those intimate and public places like the bath or Quinnsworth. Maybe it wouldn't work in Quinnsworth, it might scramble their electronic tills. I could use it on the pier though, right down at the end by the lighthouse.

195

'Excuse me,' I could say. 'Hang on a minute till I turn down the elements.'

'Hallo?'

'Could I speak please to Miss Emily Glover?'

An English voice. A secretary doing her job of work.

Emily, indeed!

'I'm afraid she isn't here at the moment. Who is speaking?'

'Jeffs, Stubbs and Warner. This is Mr Warner's secretary.'

'May I give her a message?'

'When will Miss Glover be available?'

'I'm not quite sure. Will I tell her to ring you when she comes in?'

'Mr Warner is the late Mr Glover's solicitor. He is very anxious to contact Miss Glover. Do you know when she is coming back to London?'

'I'm afraid I don't know. Does she have your number. I'll get her to ring you as soon as possible.'

'That would be the best thing.' She rattles off a telephone number and I write it down.

We mutually thank each other and I put the phone down.

Perhaps, I think, he has resurrected himself.

Perhaps God didn't want him.

Perhaps the other lot didn't want him either.

Nothing for it old chap, but to come back to earth.

Lots of the best illusionists have got themselves out of coffins six feet deep before now.

I presume the Provos did a good job though.

I pick up the phone again and ring my mother's number.

Molly answers.

'Ah,' she says when she hears my voice. 'They're at their lunch.'

'Would you give Robin a message for me please?'

'I'll get her. She's looking pale. You should tell her to mind herself a bit better.'

She puts the receiver down on the table with a clatter and I can hear her calling Robin.

'Star?'

'Sorry to bother you darling, but your father's solicitor rang.'

'Warner. What did he want?'

'To talk to you. There seemed an element of urgency.'

'I'll be back in about an hour. I'll ring him then. I've decided I'll get the seven thirty plane back home, this evening.'

'That's fine, darling.'

'Maybe Martyn's left all his money to the dogs' home.'

'That'd be a laugh.'

To give her her due, she laughs a little.

*   *   *

Dear Bill,

Thank you for your patience.

Here at last is something for you to consider. It seems like a novel, though short, to me, as I feel that a novel comes in many shapes and forms. Maybe this is too formless, and that is for you to decide. I promise I will not be either offended or angered if you don't like it, so please don't pretend anything you don't feel. Remember that it is as much your child as mine, you had the pleasure of begetting it, I, the pain of giving birth. Who'd be a woman! I look forward to hearing from you, no matter what you may have to say ... much love ...

It was several days before I heard from him. It seemed like several weeks.

I scrubbed, scoured, polished.

My mother would have approved of my gleaming house. All the time I occupied myself with this energy-consuming work a shadowy figure of a woman sat in my head, plaintively saying: 'Let me out. Please notice me. I want my freedom now.' But I didn't want to go back to the typewriter until I had heard something from Bill. So she had to remain for the time being, locked in the dark.

I cut the grass for the last time that year. I put the lawnmower away in the shed cleaned and oiled.

The wind was now starting to send little shivers of golden leaves across the grass. Sharp smoke from bonfires in the village caught from time to time in your eyes and throat.

I no longer had to collect Robin from school. She and her friends loitered and played on the way home, anything more than the most superficial parental supervision was frowned upon.

We were having to make decisions about her future.

I wanted her to go by bus each day to the grammar school in Ipswich.

Martyn had other notions.

He received glossy brochures from girls' boarding-schools all over the country which he would pass on to me when he had read them himself; Benenden, St Leonard's, St Mary's Calne, Bedales, Cheltenham Ladies College.

I barely glanced at them as it was becoming apparent that I wasn't going to have much say in the matter anyway.

'We want the best for her,' Martyn would say. 'The very best that money can buy.'

For once my mother agreed with him.

'If it hadn't been for the war, we would have sent you away to school, like the boys. It teaches you to work. Concentrates the mind. No one has ever taught you to concentrate your mind, dear.'

I couldn't argue with that.

'No harm meant. Anyway, an only child needs the company of other children. They grow up strange otherwise, don't you think?'

I presumed she was thinking of Martyn.

The house gleamed and glittered. The grass was like a bloody carpet, there wasn't a weed to be seen in any of the flowerbeds.

I couldn't read. The words jumped out of my head as soon as they made their way in.

If only there were some way of knowing, some comfortable confidence.

Why should I, after so many years, discover an aptitude?

Awful word aptitude, more applicable to hockey or maybe embroidery.

'Your daughter, Mrs Macnamara, has an aptitude for ballroom dancing.'

That of course was true. Though only I was aware of it.

I liked that aptitude.

How about . . . a hidden source of creativity? Hmmm.

A spring of ideas and words bubbling and curling inside my head and indeed sometimes my bowel.

A bit romantic.

I tended to Martyn with deference and affection and his eyes became blue and benign once more.

I was expecting Robin home from school at any minute; her sandwiches were on the kitchen table, her glass of milk poured out.

I was attempting to read a thriller, but each time I turned a page I forgot what had been written on the one before.

The telephone rang.

'Hello, sport.'

'Bill.'

I put my hand out and held onto the wall.

'We're in business. I'm sorry I didn't ring this morning, but we had a long, long meeting. Your name came up.'

'In business?'

I heard the kitchen door open and Robin hurling her schoolbag across the floor.

'Mummy!'

'Yes. Congratulations. I love it. Couldn't put it down. I was so ...'

'Mummy!'

'Shut up a minute. I'm on the phone.'

'So happy. I do have to say relieved too. I thought maybe...'

Robin came into the hall and stared at me.

'... Well, you know maybe I was wrong. But ... oh joy. Stella pulled the rabbit out of the hat. If you'll excuse that allusion. Why don't you say something?'

'I don't know what to say. I'm gobsmacked.'

'What's that? It sounds great.'

'Dumbfounded in English.'

He laughed.

'Gobsmacked. I must remember that.'

'Who are you talking to?'

'Ssssh.'

'What do you mean, sssh?'

'I wasn't talking to you. Robin is here ... I'm holding onto the wall.'

'Are you happy, sport?'

201

'I will be. In a few minutes. At the moment I know nothing. I'm just holding onto the wall. I will be happy though.'

'Who are you …? Are you crying? Mummy?'

'Shut up.'

'Lunch tomorrow, sport. This is an order. Come to the office at twelve thirty and we'll celebrate and talk business. In the meantime be brave. You're a great lady. I love you and your book. Now, go and look after your child.'

He made a lot of kissing noises down the phone.

Robin looked interested.

Click.

'Mummy.'

'Yes, darling.'

'You are crying.'

'No. Yes. Not really. I'm happy. I'm superbly happy.'

I caught her in my arms and whirled her round the hall.

'Why? Tell me why? Do stop. I'm dizzy. Tell me, tell me, tell me why.'

'The most wonderful, extraordinary, amazing, perfect thing in the whole world has just happened. I'll tell you tonight when Daddy comes home. I have to tell Daddy first.'

'Why?'

'Because it's polite to tell the person you love when something really important happens.'

'Don't you love me?'

202

'Of course I do, but he's older than you so he has to be told first.'

* * *

It was late when he came home. Robin was already in her bed and asleep.

I heard the car turn in the gateway and then stop. I heard the door slam.

I stood in the middle of the sitting-room trembling with excitement and anxiety.

He didn't come into the house, but walked round the side towards the barn. I ran out into the garden calling his name.

'Martyn. Martyn.'

The sound was like the crying of a bird.

The birds were no longer in the aviary, but were safely roosting in the barn, the door shut to keep them from harm and the possibility of frost.

He didn't seem to hear me so I called again.

'Martyn.'

He paused, his back to me, his hand on the latch.

'What is it?'

'May I talk to you for a minute? I've got something to tell you.'

'All in good time,' he said and went into the barn.

I could see the light come on and hear the sleepy murmur of surprise from the birds.

I went back into the house.

203

I took a bottle of wine from the fridge and opened it.

I poured myself a glass.

'Here's to me.'

I sat down at the table and waited for him to come in.

I waited.

I was on my third glass when he came in through the door.

A little wind came in with him and curled around my shoulders. The windows were black holes now, the lights from the kitchen reflected in them. My movements, his movements as he went to the basin and washed his hands mirrored in the dark glass.

'What's on your mind?'

He came over and put his wet hands on my shoulders. I could feel the dampness seeping through my shirt.

'Wine,' he said.

'I'm celebrating. Have some. Celebrate with me.'

'What have you to celebrate?'

'My book has been accepted.'

He took his hands from my shoulders.

'What's this? What book?'

He poured himself a glass of wine and stood looking down at me.

'I have written a book.'

I tried to keep my voice calm.

'I have been writing a book for ages. You know that. You know ... the typewriter ...'

'I didn't know you were still at that. Your secret life. I didn't realise you had such a grandiose plan in mind as to write a book. Well, well.'

'I have written a novel, Martyn. Today I have heard that it is to be published. At this moment I am celebrating ... quietly.'

He leant forward and lightly kissed the top of my head, then he sat down beside me.

'I am a little bewildered, but congratulations. Congratulations on your success and on your secrecy. I wouldn't have thought it possible to keep such a secret under your hat. But perhaps everyone else in the world knows about it except me.'

'No one knows, except the publishers. I don't really have a whole world to tell.'

'Mummy, surely? Daddy?'

'You are the first person to know. You are the only person to celebrate with me.'

'Cheers.'

'Cheers.'

He drained the glass in one and then put it very carefully down on the table.

'And the publisher? Who ...?'

'Bill. It's Bill's house has accepted it.'

'Ah. Your old pal. Jobs for the boys and all that.'

I felt my face going red.

'I wouldn't think so. There are reputations at stake.'

'Well, anyway. It's wonderful news. I am so

205

glad for you.'

He flicked his empty glass with a finger.

'Any hope of food? I'm starving.'

As I got up to get the food from the oven he gave my behind a smack.

'I'll have to mind my Ps and Qs with a lady writer around, won't I?'

'Of course,' I said.

As we ate our dinner I told him about the book.

'It's called *Lugnaquilla*.'

'Come again.'

'It's the name of a mountain in Co. Wicklow.'

'This is a book about Ireland?'

'Well, yes.'

'At least it's not about me.'

He laughed.

'Never told you anything you could write a book about, did I?'

'It's about a woman, who gets lost on the mountain in a mist and spends the night crouching under a bush waiting for the morning to come.'

'Not much of a story.'

'No.'

'What did you say the name of the mountain was?'

'Lugnaquilla ... I'll probably have to change it. No one here will know how to pronounce it. It is just a provisional title. I didn't really expect the book to be accepted.'

He was leaning back in his chair staring at the ceiling.

'I do feel very excited.'

He said nothing.

'A bit apprehensive.'

He still said nothing. I put out my hand to touch his arm and he flinched away as if he thought I was going to hit him.

'I have to go to London tomorrow.'

'Why?'

'To talk about the book. Talk about a contract. That sort of thing. Bill wants me to have lunch with him.'

'What about Robin?'

'I can take the taxi to the station and get the ten o'clock train ... Would you be able to be home by four?'

'No. I have a very busy day. I may not be home tomorrow night.'

He looked at me with a slight smile.

'I'll have to ask Elizabeth's mother to have her for tea. Quid pro quo. I've done it a million times for her.'

'I don't want Robin to be upset.'

'I don't think she'll be upset. I'll be back by seven. She'll have a great time riding Elizabeth's pony.'

*　　*　　*

The train came in to Liverpool Street and the forgotten smell of London hit me as I stepped onto the platform. It was a sharp day and dust and a few papers scurried at street corners, blown by surprising gusts of an east wind. Nothing much seemed to be changed. People were hurrying to get somewhere. No one looked happy. I felt like a visitor, which, of course, I was.

Bill was waiting for me at the restaurant, with a slim, fair man.

'Hello, sport.'

They both stood up when they saw me.

He kissed me.

'This is Peter. He's our publicity director. He likes it. We all like it. No dissension.'

Peter shook my hand.

'I like it.'

'Thank you.'

We all sat down.

We all smiled like mad things at each other.

They had serious-looking drinks in front of them, with little twists of lemon floating.

'What will you have?'

'White wine, please.'

While Bill gave the order to a waiter, Peter smiled even harder at me, and I smiled back.

My face may break, I thought, before this day is out.

'I don't know what to say.'

'Leave it to Bill. He'll say everything that needs to be said.'

Bill turned from the waiter.

'It's very good. There's no need for anxiety.

You might have been writing all your life. I gave it to the chairman this morning, but there'll be no bother from him. Like I said on the telephone, I got quite scared when it actually arrived, but two minutes into it and I knew we were flying.'

The waiter put a glass down in front of me. I held it up towards Bill and then towards Peter.

'Love you baby,' said Bill.

Peter smiled.

'We'll order. Why don't you have the most expensive thing on the menu?'

'Is that what most authors do?'

'Some. A few pick distractedly at lettuce leaves. I find that so inhibiting.'

'I won't inhibit you.'

We browsed in silence for a few minutes and ordered to Bill's satisfaction.

'He always eats as if it is to be his last meal,' said Peter.

'You never can tell. Can you? And poor old sport here has to go all the way back to Suffolk.'

He took my hand.

'We won't go through the rigmarole, welcome to the firm and all that. We'll take it as read. I know we'll have a long and happy relationship. The party of the third party and all that. Take it all as read. I'm not looking for any changes ... except the title. We need a decent, pronounceable title and we'll get to work right away. I'd like to publish in May. It will be up to Peter to see that it sells thousands of copies.'

'What name?' asked Peter.

'Name?'

'Yes. You never know with women whether they want their husband's name or their own.'

'Macnamara.'

'It has a good ring to it.'

'And you ought to get an agent. To protect your interests and keep you safe from people like Bill.'

I laughed.

'He's right,' said Bill. 'I'll give you some advice about that later. Point you in the right direction. Are you happy?'

'About this?'

He nodded.

'I feel reborn. Like I'm at the beginning of my life again, except I know how to walk and talk and . . .'

'Write,' said Peter.

'I was going to say, dance a slow foxtrot.'

'Very handy.'

'And fuck,' said Bill.

'I will ignore that . . . and I've had a child, so I've fulfilled that natural function. The decks are clear. I feel fine.'

'Hurray.'

'Is that daft?'

'Here's to cleared decks.'

We all waved our glasses in the air and Bill ordered a bottle of wine.

Peter continued to smile and say little during lunch and suddenly as Bill was about to order coffee he jumped to his feet.

'I have to fly. I have a meeting in five minutes. Sorry, sorry, sorry. Unlike Bill I have to work.'

He took my hand and held it for a moment and then surprisingly bent and kissed it.

'I'm so pleased to have met you. I hope to see you again soon, unofficially as well as officially. Goodbye.'

He put his hand on Bill's shoulder.

'Ce soir.'

Bill nodded.

'Sport.'

He watched Peter as he walked through the restaurant and went out into the street. His face was expressionless.

'Well?'

The word startled me with its abruptness.

'Peter?'

'Oh, Peter. He seems very nice. How can I say more than that? He didn't have much chance to speak. Yes. I can say, yes.'

He nodded.

'Have a glass of brandy.'

'I might fall under a bus.'

He sighed.

'We must be getting old. I used to be able to get full as a kite at lunch-time and do a long, meaningful afternoon of work. We live together. More or less in harmony. Five years

211

since we took that plunge. Old married couple. Hey, sport.'

'Are you happy?'

'I think we must love each other. It's not all roses, sport. Don't get that sentimental glaze in your eyes. We have areas of disaffection. But by and large ... I think one might call it love.'

He took a sugar lump and dipped it into his coffee. He watched as the brown spread up through the lump.

'What does the conjuror have to say about the book? He likes it, I hope?'

'He hasn't read it yet. He's not thrilled about the idea of it. I think it makes him feel a bit insecure.'

'Insecure my ass. He's just a selfish conjuror who wants to keep you safe inside his top hat with the rabbit.'

I told him the story of the fox and immediately felt guilty for having done so.

He took my hand and spread the fingers wide on the table, palm up towards him. He stared at it for a long time as if he were reading my future.

'I think you should gird yourself, sport.'

*   *   *

I went, fairly unsoberly, to Liberty after lunch and bought myself some unnecessary clothes. A long, midnight blue caftan with gold and crimson embroidery and a pair of crimson silk shoes. Thank you God, I muttered as I wrote the cheque. I'm going to be earning again. I'm going to be able to enjoy having follies once more. A pair of soft leather boots, almost knee high, that were definitely not made for walking through country fields. A dark green party dress for Robin, that they said I could change if it didn't fit. With each cheque that I wrote it seemed that a little more weight was lifted from my head. I felt irresponsible and far more cheerful than I had done for years.

I remember that afternoon of spending now and it makes me laugh just to think of it.

Before I left the shop, I went to the men's department and chose a long, fringed silk scarf for Martyn. It was shades of grey and blue, like his changing eyes.

*   *   *

It is strange the pieces of your life that float up to the surface of your mind, like the remnants of some ancient shipwreck.

It was the macabre manner of his death that created the whirlpool of memories in my head. He might have come to a sticky end sometime or other, but it is ironic that it was the virus of my country's illness that felled him.

God forgive me.

God forgive us all.

I have to keep in check the pusillanimous notion that I should explain myself to her,

213

make some sort of excuse.

I think though that she should be allowed to keep her dream of her father intact. The dream abandoned by his flighty and ambitious wife.

The loving father, his wings clipped by his responsibilities towards his child.

Generous, gift-bearing, concerned, heroic ... all done by mirrors.

She will go back to England and I will resume my normal life and we will meet at funerals, my father's, my mother's, and we will tell each other pleasantries and remember our pasts with them.

Cool. We will be cool.

I would love her to love me.

* * *

He never wore the scarf, or not anyway to my knowledge.

After he had unwrapped it he looped it carefully round his neck and went over to the mirror. He looked at himself, this way and that and then carefully took it off, folded it and put it back in its box.

'It's lovely,' he said. 'Thank you.'

I never saw it again.

I suppose he wasn't really a scarf man.

He never asked me about my day, but I got the feeling he was testing me. He was waiting for me to speak first so that he could then wound me with his indifferent replies.

My typewriter was no longer hidden. I had rearranged a corner of my bedroom as a work place. A table by the window held the machine, a stack of paper, notebooks, pencils, pens and a box with typewriter ribbons and Tippex. I also had a dictionary, the *Oxford Book of Quotations* and my old school Shakespeare.

Saturdays became the days when more and more people came to see Martyn's bird show. Sometimes they needed to be given a meal, other times they just piled out of their cars and led by Dr Rhodes they would skirt the house and head for the barn. Sometimes two or three men would remain behind after the others had left and they would stay over in the barn talking, the lights on, long after dark, or go down to the hotel.

I was never invited to watch again, but from time to time, if she had nothing better to do, Robin would slip in through the barn door behind the visitors.

Once I remember her asking him if he would do magic tricks for her birthday party.

He put out his hand and ruffled her hair.

'No, little bird. No. no.'

'Why not?'

'Because I never do anything like that without being paid for it.'

'I'll pay you.'

'You couldn't afford me. I demand...' He dropped his voice. 'A fortune.'

'Mummy could pay.'

'Only kings and queens and American millionaires can afford to pay me.'

She accepted that and nodded. There were no ill feelings. On the other hand, the day I found her in my room, tapping away on my typewriter and asked her quite politely not to do it again, there were ill feelings. She cried for twenty minutes and slammed her bedroom door and told Martyn when he came home in the evening.

'Why not? Why can't she use the damn thing if she wants to? It won't do you any harm to let her.'

'No. I wouldn't let kings or queens or even American millionaires use it and that's flat.'

Neither of them laughed.

I obviously didn't have the right touch.

* * *

My mother wrote me a letter when she heard about the book.

She always writes with a fat nib fountain pen and she uses blue Quink ink. Always the same. The letters sit neatly on the page, well formed and eminently legible. I have that letter still, somewhere in the bottom of a drawer.

My dear Stella, Your father and I are so happy to hear that this book you have written is to be published. I have felt for a long time that whatever talents you have

216

were being wasted, tucked away as you are in the depths of the English countryside. I wonder to myself where this particular talent has come from, as far as I know there have never been literary people on either side of the family. Your father had a great-aunt who tried unsuccessfully to emulate Lord Tennyson; she merely wasted a lot of paper and some very black ink. I am glad to see that you have found something to do with your life that is truly your own. Life and the opportunities to live it fully have so changed from my young days. I would like to have been a doctor, but they all suggested that I should become a nurse ... not the same thing at all. Sensibly, I think, I turned my nose up at their suggestion. This, of course, doesn't mean that I haven't been very happy looking after your father and bringing up you children, but there have been times in the darkness of the night and insomnia, when I have wished that I had had the courage to defy the people who loved me and take some risks. Other women of my age did, and I have admired them for it. I never thought I would write such a letter to anyone, but perhaps you can say things to writers that you would not say to anyone else, even daughters!

I hope that this will be the first of many books and that you will find success and happiness in your life.

Your loving mother.
PS Molly sends her love. When I told her the news she put on one of her brooding looks and said I knew that girl would pull something out of her hat one day. Not, I thought, quite the right thing to say given your husband's propensity for conjuring tricks.

We have never mentioned this letter in all the years since it was sent.

*   *   *

I used to wonder, after I had left him, if the bird performance was not really a front for something else. Something nefarious; guns or drugs perhaps, something that took him to the strange and dangerous parts of the world in which he and his birds and Dr Rhodes and Peter Magill travelled most; parts of the world where there were no kings and queens or American millionaires.

It was certainly a powerful act, but was one such act enough to make all that travelling worth while? Where did all his money come from? Did he move from the petty dealing in which I had often felt he might be involved to something altogether more dangerous?

Was, in fact, his death the terrible accident that it was thought to be?

Presumably Dr Rhodes and Peter Magill are

218

the only people who know the answer to such questions? Or were they merely part of his illusionist's bag of tricks; their minds too filled with lights, mirrors, birds, effects to see some other agenda?

I wonder will Robin let the birds fly free now that she has presumably inherited them.

Will she open the aviary and watch them take to the sky?

Maybe they will be safer where they are. They might become instant prey to predators, those delicious corn-fed doves.

*   *   *

'Why do you stay with the conjuror, sport?'

We had been talking about the approaching launch of the book and were sitting in his office drinking coffee, before I left to catch the train home.

'I have no reason to leave him. He doesn't ill-treat me. I have no other man in my life. We have a child. Lots of reasons like that.'

He looked at me thoughtfully.

'Love?'

'Not any longer. I feel uneasy with him, guilty that I haven't lived up to his expectations.'

'What were they?'

I shook my head.

'I don't remember. I presume at one stage we both had expectations. They seem to have

219

got lost.'

'I see him from time to time, you know, round about Kensington Church Street.'

He paused.

'Popping in and out of shops there. Just round the corner from our flat. From time to time I see him.'

'So?'

I got up.

He stood up. always the gentleman, Bill.

'I'm just giving you a piece of information. I don't think he has ever seen me.'

He held my coat for me.

He picked up my bag from the floor and held it out towards me.

'Big day, next week. You don't need to worry, the feedback is good. You know, from booksellers and all that.'

He crossed the room and held the door open for me. He put his hand on my shoulder as I walked past him.

'What I'm really trying to say, sport, is that he is never alone when I see him. From time to time.'

He kissed my cheek.

'I presumed that was what you were trying to say.'

*   *   *

His presents now were all for Robin.

I watched his seduction of her and

remembered his seduction of me.

She would listen for the sound of the car and her face would become alive, expectant when she heard him opening the hall door. I was nothing to her, merely the person who kept her life running smoothly. Her radiance was all for him.

I was too preoccupied with my work to counter this state of affairs. I only wanted equilibrium. I never for a moment thought I was neglecting her, I simply was aware that I didn't have as much to offer her as he did.

He barely spoke to me, except to give me orders from time to time, perhaps tell me of his immediate plans ... and of course his plans for Robin. His views on Robin's future were unyielding, my arguments without any health in his eyes.

I remember once suggesting that if he really insisted that she should go to boarding-school that he might consider sending her to Ireland.

He looked at me with astonishment. 'Why on earth?'

'She is, after all, half Irish. You always seem to forget that in your deliberations.'

'Oh God, I pray she will never be burdened with that weight on her back. After all, her future, her career, her successes will be here in this country. In England.'

'Have you taken up prophecy as well as conjuring?'

'Don't let's have any more nonsense about

221

this. She's going to be assured, sure of who she is and proud of it.'

'Like you?'

'You know nothing about me.'

'It's not for want of trying. Your life is a well-guarded secret.'

'Prying, I would call it. Remember, curiosity killed the cat.'

'Call it what you like.'

'It's the way I see it. Always looking for things about me to despise.'

'That's not fair. I have never wanted to despise you. Share burdens. We all have burdens.'

'I have no burdens and I want to make sure that Robin has no burdens either, so it's best if you don't manufacture them for her.'

'I just want her to have a decent education that reflects her background. You seem to want to elevate her to some dizzy height she may not be able to handle.'

'The best is all I want for her and the best is what she'll have.'

There wasn't much more to say.

* * *

Two days before the book launch a man arrived with a green van and a large number of birds were caged and safely stowed on the shelves. I watched from the windows as the three men walked backwards and forwards

222

across the grass, carrying the cages in their hands with care. The birds were silent.

As the driver carefully closed and locked the doors, Martyn came into the house. I heard him running up the stairs. After a short while he came down carrying a case.

'Are you going away?'

'What does it look like? A week. We have an engagement in Holland.'

'How wonderful. Why didn't you tell me?'

'I didn't think you'd be interested.'

He walked towards the door.

'I had hoped you would be coming to my launch.'

'It never occurred to me. Even if I had been here, I don't think I would have come.'

'Oh.'

'It's quite impossible. I'm going to be in Holland. I'm sorry.'

'Well...'

We stood looking at each other for quite a long time.

'Good luck,' I said eventually.

He nodded and walked out the door.

'What about me?' I called after him. 'What about wishing me good luck?'

He got into his car and slammed the door.

He drove off down the road, followed by the green van.

Dust rose and hovered in the air and then settled once more on the road, the sound of the cars faded away.

My mother and father came over from Dublin for the launch. It was a modest, agreeable affair; a few literary editors, who mainly talked to each other, some friendly critics, a handful of Bill's other writers, a bookseller or two, several of the staff from the office.

My mother and father sensibly arrived late, smiled a lot and had dinner with Bill, Peter and myself afterwards. It was anticlimactic. I was tired in my head and in my body. In typically English fashion no one mentioned the book.

During dinner the four of them discussed Ireland, Irish politics, Irish history, Irish literature. I half listened, the smile from the launch still on my face and thought how splendid it was to come from a place that generates so much chat and I thought of Robin and hoped that she was all right staying with her friend Caroline, and I wondered if I should have brought her up with me. To hell with school, this was a momentous occasion! I thought about Martyn and wondered where he was, what part of Holland with the green van and Peter Magill's lights and the white doves, wings folded, in their little cages. I wondered if doves got seasick, but presumed they probably didn't.

Bill nudged me.

'You must be tired, sport?'

I nodded.

'You'll get used to this sort of thing.'

My mother leaned across the table.

'We want to buy twenty-seven copies of Stella's book. Will you let us have a discount?'

I blushed.

Bill hooted with laughter.

'Trade discount. No problem. I'll get them posted off to you first thing tomorrow.'

'It's not every day ... you know. We all have to do our bit. Very few of our friends buy books ... they read them you know, but they seldom, if ever, buy them. I have to admit to using the library mostly myself. We are life members of the RDS.'

She paused.

She made sure that we were all listening.

'That is the Royal Dublin Society. I don't imagine you've ever heard of it. I suppose one day they will remove the word Royal. Personally, I think that would be a pity, not, you understand, for political reasons, I am no lover of kings and queens, forgive me if I offend you in any way, but for reasons of history. Our history has removed from us the need for kings or queens. We do have good bits of history as well as bad bits Mr ... ahh ...'

'Do call me Bill.'

'Bill. Thank you. Yes. I'd like to do that.'

She smiled benignly round the table and I realised that she was drunk ... well not seriously drunk, but in that state of having had several more drinks than she might normally

225

have at home, or even out to dinner with friends.

'Bill.' She repeated the name again and then turned her smiling face towards Peter.

'I am so sorry. I am so bad at remembering.'

'Peter,' he said.

She nodded.

'Should be easy enough to remember, but I find names are like butterflies. Hard to trap. You have both been so kind to Stella. My husband and I would like to thank you for that. She hasn't much sense.'

Bill hooted with laughter again and waved his hand for the waiter.

'You never said a truer word. Shall we all have brandy? Or would you, dear Mrs Macnamara, prefer something more exotic?'

'Yes,' said my mother. 'Benedictine. A large Benedictine on the rocks.'

'Mother...'

My father put his hand on my arm.

'Leave her be, Stella. She's having a wonderful time. She hasn't let rip for ages. We've all got horribly set in our ways. I have to thank you for creating the opportunity for us to unbend a little.'

'Hear, hear,' said my mother. 'It's so lucky that Ben and Katie aren't here. That's my eldest son and his wife. She never lets a drop pass her lips, or his if she can manage it. Quite difficult to handle sometimes. Not of course that we ... that we ... you must understand ...

you do understand, don't you?'

'I understand,' said Bill, pushing glasses furiously round the table.

'A very good girl ... well woman I should say. Very good. Keeps Ben on the straight and narrow. She doesn't read. No time she says. She's too busy. Children you know. Of course, most people don't read, do they? ... Have you met Martyn?'

'Well ...'

Luckily another thought entered her head.

'And you two nice boys, where have you hidden your wives this evening?'

'No wives, Mrs Macnamara. God has not seen fit to send us wives.'

'I don't see what God has to do with it.'

'Forgive me. I thought the Irish saw the hand of God in everything.'

She laughed.

'Maybe we seem like that to the outside world, but really it's the other way round you know, we tell God what to do. We are his major advisers ... so if it's wives you're looking for let me know and I'll get on to the man above about it.'

She looked at him for a long time in silence with a slight smile on her face.

'But I don't suppose you need anything apart from what you've already got.'

'I like your mother,' said Bill.

'Isn't this a happy evening? I do like a really happy evening.'

227

I hear Robin's key in the door.

I have really very little idea how she lives over there or with whom she lives.

She is like her father, she tells me only the minimum.

I presume that is my fault.

I didn't fight for her.

It never occurred to me to force her to come with me to Dublin. She seemed so adamant in her desire to stay with Martyn.

'They're getting so old. I can't bear to sit there looking at them pretending they can hear you, pretending nothing has changed, pretending they're not disintegrating.'

She stood just inside the door. Her voice was angry.

'They are old, darling. The alternative is death. You should be glad they're still there, not angry.'

'I hate feeling helpless. I want to know that they'll be there for ever and when I see them like that I know they won't. I hate that. I don't know what to say to them. Grandfather's so deaf he never hears anything you say and Granny wants to know all sorts of things I don't want to tell her. She's like the Spanish Inquisition.'

'They love you.'

'I suppose so. Maybe Daddy was right. He didn't need that sort of baggage. I don't think I do either. I just keep thinking of more bloody funerals. And with each funeral, your own comes closer. Don't you ever feel death hovering behind you?'

'Not very often.'

'Well, you should. Look what happened to Daddy.'

She takes a cigarette from her pocket and holds it in her right hand as she gropes for her lighter.

'I've no one now to protect me,' she says suddenly. 'I don't suppose you ever have that feeling of total vulnerability. Sometimes I feel as if I were made of glass and if someone bumped against me I would shatter into a million pieces.'

She gestures around the room with the cigarette, as if the floors, the chairs and tables were all covered with fine slivers of glass.

'I bet you've never felt anything like that.'

There is almost an accusation in her voice.

'No. I haven't. I'm a tough old boot.'

'Yes, he always said that you were in love with yourself. He said that frequently. It was your major problem.'

I shut my mouth on the words that want to tumble out and go across the room and put my arms around her.

'Darling, maybe I can protect you a little.'

'I doubt it,' she says.

* * *

He stands, arms outstretched, weighted down it seems with doves.

The tremor of their wings gives an urgency to the image.

He is quite still, quite unperturbed by their agitation.

He stands.

After a moment or two they settle into a sleepy torpor, almost it seems as if they had been drugged.

The lights dim and as they do he begins to move his arms slowly up and down.

As he moves the wings tremble.

The movement of his arms becomes faster and the wings of the birds move rhythmically with the movement of the man's arms.

Bright lights begin to sweep the stage and as we watch the man bird rises above us into the darkness and becomes an angel. You can feel the cold wind as the huge wings beat in the air.

The lights change their colour and flames lick upwards as the angel strives to burst away from the danger, burst through the roof out into the world.

A woman screams.

As the flames sink the lights dim and then there is only blackness.

After what seems like only a moment the lights come up again and the stage is empty, only a feather or two drift in the air.

*   *   *

I took Robin and two of her friends up to see him in the Chiswick Empire.

We went up in the train which the children loved and he was going to drive us home after the show.

His act was the grand finale. He came after tap dancers, stand-up comedians, a man dressed as a pearly king who sang 'My old man said follow the van, and don't dilly dally on the way', a conjuror, three dancing dogs and several spangled trapeze artists.

It was a Saturday night and the audience was enthusiastic.

The girls were wild.

'Is that really your Daddy?' One of them asked Robin as we headed for the exit.

Robin nodded. Her eyes were shining with excitement and when we met Martyn in the foyer, she clung to his arm like one of the doves. He ruffled her hair and hugged her.

It was dark as we walked down Chiswick High Road towards the car and there was a slice of new moon in the sky. He swung Robin round on the pavement and caught the hand of one of her friends.

'Turn your money in your pocket,' he sang. 'Whenever you see a new moon.'

The three of them danced and scampered and the passers-by watched them for a moment and laughed.

He let go of the girls' hands and, continuing to dance on his own, produced from the air gold- and silver-wrapped chocolates which he threw to the children and the watchers. The girls screamed with delight.

He never threw anything in my direction, not even one of his charming smiles.

*   *   *

'You'd better ring the solicitor,' I say to her.

She nods but doesn't move. I feel her weight in my arms, as if I were carrying her, the dead warm weight of her. My arms feel stretched with the weight of her. Her breath smells of cigarettes and red wine.

I say nothing.

I am so afraid that I will say the wrong words.

I am afraid.

I would love to dance with her around this room; a gentle, slow dance that would say the words I am afraid to say. After a moment she steps away from me. My arms follow her and then fall by my side, trembling with the weight they have carried.

'Yes,' she says.

For a moment I can't remember why she said yes, and then I do.

'I'll put the kettle on and make a cup of tea, while you...'

'The boring thing about Ireland is that everybody's always making cups of tea. I'd much rather have a gin and tonic.'

'I'll get you one.'

'Don't bother. I was only joking. But I don't want a cup of tea either.'

She picks up the telephone from the hall table and carries it into her bedroom and closes the door.

* * *

He took Robin skiing one Christmas holidays. Just for a week.

'I feel I need to get to know her,' he said to me. 'Alone. Anyway you wouldn't enjoy it.'

'How do you know?'

'You don't enjoy anything. You spread your sourness round the place. It would be good for her to get away from that for a while.'

'Thanks,' I said.

They apparently had a wonderful time.

'Daddy says I'm a natural skier,' she said in the bath the night after they had come home. 'He's going to take me again some time. You should have come. I drank wine for my dinner and stayed up till ten o'clock. He said what was the point of holidays if you couldn't stay up late. He went out with his friends after I was in bed. He said I was quite safe because the chambermaid was keeping an eye on me.'

'His friends?'

'I forget really.' She submerged herself.

* * *

233

He paid the bills; kept me in the style to which I had grown accustomed, but he passed in and out of the house like a stranger. He never told me where he was going or when he was coming back. From time to time he telephoned to Robin from distant parts of the world. She was quite silent about his calls, only giving out monosyllabic answers to my questions.

When he came home it was for Robin he called; Robin to whom he gave presents. It was Robin's bed he sat on when he wanted to talk. I became a nobody, an invisibility. He seldom spoke to me, unless he wanted me to do something for him or to criticise in some way my behaviour.

'You weren't in when Robin came home from school yesterday.'

'I was only down at the shop, I forgot to get bread.'

'I don't want her coming into an empty house.'

'Five minutes.'

'I tell you, I don't want her coming into an empty house.'

'How many times have I told you not to get frozen chickens.'

'It isn't a frozen chicken.'

'Well it tastes like one.'

'There are no socks in my drawer.'

'Red doesn't suit you.'

My happy moments became the brief times I spent in London with Bill and Peter.

Writing became more and more my real life. The only voices that I heard most days were the voices in my head; urgent voices needing to come out from their prison and be heard.

It seemed so strange to live mainly in the imagination, to talk mainly to the unreal, to give birth over and over again to phantoms, but that was the way it became.

There was nothing I could do to make Martyn see me again. His cold grey eyes held nothing but boredom when he looked towards me, boredom and a strange anger as if in some way he had been duped.

I had finished my second novel and it was shortly to be published when Bill rang me one day.

'We're going to Venice next week, sport. Why don't you come with us? Break out.'

I laughed.

'No joke intended. I mean it. Seven days, back in time for your launch. Glorious, misty autumn in Venice.'

'I couldn't,' I said. 'Oh God, I'd love to, but I couldn't.'

'I'll give you twenty-four hours to make up your mind. We would love it ... both of us. You would make our holiday special. It would be good for you. You need to break out, you know. Ever been to Venice?'

'No...'

'I thought not. Think about it. After all, you'll be perfectly safe with us. I'll ring you tomorrow.'

He made little kissing noises and put down the phone.

I wondered if I had a valid passport.

I wondered what I could do with Robin.

I wondered what Martyn would say.

In the end of all he said nothing.

He stared at me across the table.

'Why do you want to go to Venice?'

'I've always wanted to go there. The beautiful, romantic, sinking city of the Doges.'

'Rot,' he said. 'It smells. It's falling down. It's jammed full of tourists, you'll hate that. Anyway it will be cold and dank at this time of year.'

'You know it?'

He didn't answer. He cut a roast potato neatly in two and put one half in his mouth.

He waited for me to speak.

'I think I'd like to see it for myself.'

'Suit yourself. I wouldn't dream of stopping you doing anything you wanted to do. I won't be able to take time off to mind the child though.'

'The weekend perhaps?'

'I wouldn't count on it.'

'I'll ask Elizabeth's mother if she could have her for the week. We've had Elizabeth lots of nights.'

'Whatever you see fit.'

'I don't suppose she'll mind. I think Robin would be happy there, don't you?'

He stared past me and didn't say anything.

'Of course she would,' I answered myself. 'Very happy.'

'Soon she'll be in boarding-school and you'll be able to go rushing round the world to your heart's content.'

'I just want to go to Venice, for heaven's sake. Seven days. I want to get away from here. Breathe.'

'You won't be able to breathe in Venice at this time of year, or see, if it comes to that. What's wrong with being here anyway? There's nothing...'

'Yes. That's what it is. The nothingness. I want to get away from that. Something must exist. Somewhere. I'll ring Mrs Chapman and if it's all right with her, I'll go. If not...'

I put down my knife and fork and went out to the telephone. When I came back to tell him that Mrs Chapman seemed quite happy about the whole thing, he was reading a book and didn't look up.

* * *

I can hear her voice but not the words, coming from the bedroom, like distant background music.

Perhaps secrets will now be revealed that never were during his life.

I am such a fool.

What do those secrets matter?

237

To me they became a hurdle that I was incapable of crossing; to her they are nothing. Her father was enough for her, as he stood up. One man in a million.

*　　　*　　　*

It was in Venice that Bill said to me, 'Leave him, sport. Get out while the going is good. Otherwise you'll wake up one day and find yourself mad.'

I laughed.

'Your mother agrees with me.'

'You mean you've talked to my mother about me and Martyn?'

'Actually, yes. She rang me up and said she was worried about you.'

'God, but you're a pair of interfering bastards!'

'Not at all. We love you, sport. Don't we Peter?'

Peter took my hand and kissed it.

The mist was all around us.

Buildings and people wrapped in grey, the sound of footsteps echoing and the splash of the water lapping against stone walls. Words were carried away, lost in the streams of mist. We held hands in the streets. We hugged each other in the dim doorways of churches. At night before going to bed each of them would kiss me on each cheek and then they would go together, touching lightly, shoulder to shoulder up the stairs to their room.

Amen.

*   *   *

I wanted to go home.

I wanted to bring my child home.

I wanted her to recognise the city as I recognised it. I wanted her to feel a part of a community, not just flotsam, floating on the edge of other people's lives.

I wanted all sorts of daft things.

Or maybe they weren't daft.

My mother invited us over for Christmas.

'You go if you want,' Martyn said. 'Robin and I can manage on our own. Can't we, darling?'

Robin looked at me, alarmed.

'Us,' I said. 'She invited us. Not me. Us.'

I could feel the tears thickening my voice.

'What's wrong with staying here?'

'Nothing. I was just telling you that she invited...'

'Well thank her, but we'd rather stay here. Be at home. Wouldn't we?'

'Ireland's boring,' said Robin.

'See?' he said.

'OK. You win.'

'It's a democratic decision,' said Robin, who was at the clever age.

*   *   *

That was the last Christmas.

He sparkled and shone.

When we went for drinks to the Chapmans', his hands were flying through the air, brooches, bracelets, earrings, all shining suns, moons, stars, appeared from nowhere; children and adults smiled and clapped his magic generosity. Hair clips, pencils, rings, baubles shimmered and flew.

He was like some modern Father Christmas, no reindeer, no sack on his back, no scrambling down sooty chimneys, just the outstretching of his gifted hands.

'I do love your daddy,' Elizabeth whispered to Robin.

'Yes.'

Robin basked in his reflected glory.

He brought two of the doves into the house just before dinner.

He held them clasped in his hands against his chest as he came in the kitchen door.

'Oh, Martyn. No!'

He ignored me and walked into the hall.

'Robin,' he called.

As she came running down the stairs, he held out his hands towards her and the doves were free.

He had powdered them with gold dust and as they moved their wings the air was filled with trailing gold.

She stopped on the stairs and held out her hands and the birds hovered for a moment and then gently settled on her open palms. For a moment she was haloed by golden air.

'Daddy.'

'Darling.'

I felt the terrible, unreasonable fear rising in me and I ran back into the kitchen and closed the door.

After a few minutes Robin followed me in.

'Can I carry anything for you?'

'May I . . . Where are the birds?'

'It's quite all right. You shouldn't be so silly. They won't come near you. Daddy has them totally under control.'

'I would rather he put them outside.'

She shook her head.

'They won't do you any harm.'

In the dining-room, all decorated with holly and candles, ribbons and great swags of ivy, Martyn sat in his chair at the table, with a dove on each shoulder, their heads tucked down against his neck. They never stirred throughout the meal, never made a sound. From time to time he would put up a finger and stroke one or other of them. He would look across the table as he did this, daring me to say a word.

*   *   *

It was a cold winter.

Grey day followed grey day. The landscape was forlorn.

241

The birds seldom came out into the aviary and when they did they flew disconsolately from perch to perch as if to exercise their wings and then they would huddle against each other again for warmth.

One morning towards the end of January I was awakened by a startling silence and looking out of the window found the garden covered with snow. A cold full moon hung in the sky and the sheet of white glimmered over the ground.

I went downstairs and put on my coat and my boots and went out of the back door.

It was just beginning to get light and the undersides of the clouds were slightly stained with colour. The silence was intense. As I walked I sank almost to my knees in untouched powdery snow. The cold air stung its way into my lungs as I breathed. The trees, hedges, the barn, the house were like white sculptures. The lights shining from the kitchen window made brilliant patterns on the grass.

I scooped up a handful of snow and rubbed it over my face, then clamping a ball of it in my hand I moved to below Robin's window.

'Robin,' I called up to her. 'Yoohoo, Robin, Robin.'

After a moment or two her window opened and I threw the snowball up. It missed her, splattering on the wall beside her window.

'Oh, Mummy. Oh, snow! How brilliant. Hang on a tick and I'll be down.'

I heard her feet thundering on the stairs, then the door opened and she came rushing out into the garden, barefoot and in her nightdress. She ran past me. She twirled and jumped and rolled, like some excited animal. Every part of her was soon covered with clinging snow. She scooped up handfuls and tossed them in the air, she laughed and shouted. Suddenly she stopped and stood quite still, then threw herself into my arms.

'I'm frozen,' she said.

'You mad creature, of course you are.'

I picked her up and staggered back into the house with her. In the kitchen, water and snow dripped from both of us onto the floor. Lumps of snow clung in her hair, her nightdress was sodden.

'Scurry, scurry,' I said. 'Up into the bath. I'll make us both a huge breakfast. Run, before you turn into a pillar of ice.'

On her way up the stairs, she called back to me, 'Do I need to go to school?'

'Of course you do.'

'Mean.'

'Think of the fun you'll have.'

'I bet they won't let us.'

I heard her turning on the taps.

I had really enjoyed that fifteen minutes.

'What the hell are you doing?' he shouted from his room, as Robin banged the bathroom door. 'Don't you know what the time is?'

'Get up and look out of your window.

There's wonderful snow. Mummy and I have been out rolling in it.'

Robin and I had almost finished our breakfast when he appeared in the kitchen.

'Why didn't you call me earlier? I'll have to take the train.'

I got up and took his breakfast from the oven and put the plate down at his place.

'What's this?'

I didn't answer.

'I haven't time for breakfast.'

'If you embark on the great trek, it may be the last decent meal you'll get today.'

'Mummy says I have to go to school, but I can go in my track suit.'

'Have some tea?'

He walked over to the window and stared out.

'Do you have to go to London?'

'Of course I have to go.'

'There's your tea. Will I make you some toast?'

'You'll have to come with me to the station and drive the car home.'

'No,' I said. 'I won't drive in that.'

'Daddy, if you don't want your sausages, can I have them?'

'May I.'

'May I?'

He sat down abruptly and began to eat his breakfast.

I made some fresh toast.

'You could call the taxi,' I suggested.

He didn't say anything.

'You could drive yourself. I'm sure the motorway will have been cleared. You could stay at home and spend the day on the telephone. Or as a last resort, if life is too unbearable, you could do a Captain Oates.'

'Who is Captain Oates?' asked Robin.

As I was telling her, he ate his breakfast without speaking.

He ate his sausages, his bacon, his lightly fried egg and two squares of fried bread. He drank his tea and was just buttering some toast when the telephone rang.

I stood up.

'I'll get it.'

He was up and out of the room.

After a moment he returned.

'It's Elizabeth.'

'Oh hurray. I bet she has a plan.'

He walked to the window again, rattling the keys and the coins in his pocket.

'Have you decided what to do?'

'Of course I've decided what to do.'

Jangle, jangle.

'Will you tell me?'

'I'll take the twelve o'clock train. I'll get the taxi to take me to the station and I won't be back tonight. I'll be needing the telephone when the child gets off it. God, I hate an Irish fry-up. It makes me feel bloated.'

'Thanks for telling me. Personally I thought

it was what is called a good old-fashioned English breakfast.'

Robin rushed in full of plans. Elizabeth's plans to go tobogganing after school, her plan to build a giant snowman, boots, anoraks, gloves and hot drinks in thermos flasks all came pouring out of her mouth.

Martyn went to use the telephone and spoke in low, urgent monosyllables.

'Can I bring lots of people back to tea?'

'How many is lots?'

'Anyway four. We're going to build this ginormous snowman. Bigger than a human ... like a monster. A huge monster, in the garden. Elizabeth says our garden is more suitable, because we've no flower beds. Won't that be great and we can invite everyone in the village to come and look at it and we'll charge them.'

'I don't really think you should do that. Invite them by all means. I wouldn't charge them if I were you.'

'But you're not me, are you? Elizabeth and I think we should charge sixpence a head.'

'It's an awful lot of money.'

'It's going to be a very big snow monster. We're going to have worked very hard to build it. Daddy would call it initiative.'

'Probably. What will you do if it thaws in the night?'

She looked at me rather pityingly.

'You win some, you lose some. I have to go. Elizabeth has a whole pile of snowballs hidden behind her hedge. We're going to throw them at everyone, before we go to school.'

'Wrap up well. Bring some dry clothes with you. Don't get too cold.'

How boring mothers can be!

He spent a long time on the telephone and then went out to check on the birds. I watched him cross the garden in his snow boots and his long mackintosh.

He left deep tracks behind him, snow monster tracks.

I was in the bath when the telephone rang.

I got out and wrapped myself in a towel and dripped into the bedroom.

'Yes?'

'Angela?'

'I'm afraid you have the wrong number.'

'Ah,' said the voice and rang off.

I stayed beside the phone, blotting at myself with the towel thinking a jumble of thoughts. I remembered Angela who cried at our wedding; silly memory really, her face had been pink and streaked with tears. I had handed her my flowers.

Silly memory.

Lots of people cry at weddings.

As I had expected, the phone rang again. I let it ring a few times before I answered it.

'Yes?'

'May I please speak to Martyn Glover?'

'He's out in the aviary at the moment. May I ask him to call you back?'

'Would you get him for me now? I can hold on.'

'It will take quite a while. I'm not dressed at the moment.'

'I don't mind waiting.'

'Can you give me your name please?'

'It's Dr Rhodes.'

'Oh, good morning Dr Rhodes. This is Stella. Not Angela. I'll get him for you when I've put on some clothes. Stella. Remember me?'

There was no sound from the other end.

I laid the receiver down on the table and put on some jeans and a woolly.

I ran downstairs and as I passed the phone in the hall, I picked it up.

'Don't lose heart, Dr Rhodes, I'll have him for you before you can spell Angela.'

It wasn't really very funny, but I laughed my way into the kitchen where I put on my socks and boots and then I went out into the snow for the second time that day.

It was freezing quite hard and the snow crackled as I stepped into it.

The twiggy marks of bird steps meandered round the bushes.

I must put out bread, I thought.

Martyn was standing in the aviary. In his hands he held one of the grain boxes and about fifteen birds were perched around the edge, others hovered and fluttered just above his head, waiting to see what he was going to do.

'Martyn,' I called to him.

He didn't stir.

'Martyn.'

'What is it?'

'Telephone.'

'For heaven's sake, Star, I can't come to the telephone now. Why didn't you tell whoever it is to ring again?'

'It's Dr Rhodes. He won't take no for an answer.'

He put his hand into the box and scattered grain on the snow around his feet. The birds swooped down, struggling on the ground to find the grains. He scattered more in a wide circle and they spread out, their heads bobbing up and down as they pecked and strutted, pecked again. Against the snow, their whiteness was dimmed.

'What'll I say?'

'Tell him I'm coming, of course.'

Back in the hall, I picked up the telephone once more.

'He's coming.'

There was again total silence from the other end.

'He is just feeding the birds and then he's coming. Goodbye Dr Rhodes.'

I went into the kitchen and switched on a lot of machines.

I was sitting at the kitchen table reading the paper when he came in to the room. The dishwasher, the washing machine and the radio played their various tunes. He stormed across the room and turned off the radio.

'What is this?' he shouted at me.

He was dressed for London and had a leather briefcase in his hand.

'Have a cup of coffee?'

'Rhodes said you were rude to him.'

'Well, I thought he was a bit rude to me. He insisted that I go and fetch you, even though I wasn't dressed and he called me Angela. Who is Angela?'

'How the hell should I know who Angela is?'

'I think you know very well.'

He slammed the briefcase down on the table and bent over me.

'I won't put up with this you know.'

'Put up with what?'

'Your constant lack of trust. Your ridiculous desire for irrelevant information. It's like an obsession with you. Yes. An obsession. It's ruining our lives. Yes.'

He stepped away from me, as if he couldn't bear the proximity another moment.

'What is marriage?'

He walked away from me, his head bent.

I didn't know whether to answer his question or not.

I took the safe path and remained silent.

After a moment or two he turned and looked at me. There were tears brimming in his eyes.

'I wanted love, a family, safety. I needed safety. I thought ...'

He stopped speaking and stared at me.

I poured myself another cup of coffee.

'I thought I would be safe with you. How foolish I was.'

'I don't think I can handle this,' I said.

'You see.' He spread his hands wide. 'You make jokes. You mock me.'

'I don't mean to mock you. I just don't know what to say. I have tried, believe me.'

'You're not normally at a loss for words.'

'I don't want to say the wrong thing, Martyn. These sort of intemperate conversations can be quite damaging.'

He walked across to the table and picked up his briefcase.

'You have already done the damage. Broken faith with me and now I watch with great anxiety to see if you're going to damage my child.'

'Our child.'

'I have to go.'

He walked towards the door, his back stooped a little, his right hand clenched round the handle of his briefcase, his left hand hanging limp and dispirited by his side.

'When will you be back?'

He turned at the door.

'How the hell do I know when I'll be back. How the hell do I know when I'll get where I'm going. This is my home. I'll be back when I want to be back. I'll go out when I want to go out. I don't have to give you my life history every time I move.'

I remained silent.

He stood waiting for me to say something.

'You realise, don't you, that all this nonsense is because I asked you who Angela is?'

'I told you. I know no one called Angela.'

'I don't believe you.'

'That's the second time in ten minutes you've called me a liar.'

'Probably.'

'Why do you...'

'Because in ten minutes you've told me two lies. Because in ten years you've never told me the truth. Because I'm sick and tired of pretending I believe every word you say to me. There's a whole lot more becauses, but you're in a hurry to get away so I'll keep them for another time. Now go to hell, or Dr Rhodes or Angela, I don't care which.'

He slammed the briefcase against the wall and went out leaving the hall door wide open and the wind carrying snow with it set the rugs on the hall floor rippling and banged the kitchen door in my face.

I sat and listened to him start the car and the revving of the engine as he drove through the snow in the drive and out of the gate. I sat for a long time and the bright snow fell again and covered the tracks in the garden made by the birds and the silly human beings and there was no sound only the sound of grief keening in my head, and anger.

I wonder now about that grief, which then seemed profound. I suppose it was to do with the discovery of my own weakness. It certainly wasn't the death of love that made me cry; but hope, perhaps, not that love would revive like the Phoenix, but that the unit we had created might survive. I still wonder, even after all these years alone and with no reason for grief, why we continue to feel that terrible sense of failure if the glue holding the unit together melts and the separate pieces float on the wind, this way and that way, always drifting further and further apart.

What it came to was that I had loved the illusions, but not the illusionist ... not enough anyway. And what is enough anyway when it comes to love?

There is no enough.

None of this I realised at that moment. I just felt the enormous grief of failure.

*   *   *

I had not realised that things could be over so quickly.

He came home three days later.

The snow had melted and the roads were covered with muddy slime. The fields were grey and a fierce wind blew from the east, bending the trees and hedges and howling into the house every time a door was opened. The birds were huddled on their perches or in small groups on the ground, trying to find warmth in closeness.

Robin was in the dumps, lethargic and black humoured.

'When's Daddy coming back?'

'Darling, I don't know.'

'And I bet you don't care.'

'That's cheeky. You know I don't like you being cheeky.'

'You're mean to him.'

'That's a matter of opinion.'

'It's my opinion. It's his opinion too. I observe, you know. Miss Hailwood says I am a most observant person.'

Miss Hailwood was flavour-of-the-month teacher.

'Well, there you go.'

'What does that mean? That's the sort of thing you say to Daddy. I've heard you.'

'It only means that I am at a loss for words.'

'How can a writer be at a loss for words?'

'It's the easiest thing in the world. Perhaps that's why they write. That's their way to find words. Wrap up well if you're going out, that wind is like a knife.'

'I'm just going to help ... feed the birds.'

'Wrap up ...'

'I heard you the first time.'

She was in the hall putting on her coat when he came in. I heard their voices, her joyful laughter, their steps on the floor, the door bang and after a moment I watched through the window as they walked arm in arm across the grass towards the barn.

She laughed at something he said, and he pulled her close against him. I wondered what they were talking about.

I knew that I was going to have to go.

Home.

Mother.

What would Mother have to say to me?

I poured myself a glass of wine.

Dutch courage.

'I'm sorry, I really am sorry, I have to go. Mother. I really am sorry, this is not what you would have wanted, Mother. But it's not what I would have wanted either. I hope you believe me.'

The telephone rang.

I didn't answer it.

I stared out of the window at the wind, with the glass in my hand and the dissonance of the phone grated in my head.

I have to go.

I want to go.

I'm sorry.

Honestly I am.

Mother.

Why do I live up to no one's expectations?

* * *

It took me three days to tell him.

He was at home all that time.

He only came into the house for meals.

He spoke only to Robin, or obliquely through her to me.

After school she would go straight out to the barn and not come in until I called them for their supper.

They would come hand in hand, smiling, across the sodden grass and as they came in the kitchen door the smiles would be switched from their faces.

They washed their hands in silence and sat down at the kitchen table.

'Goulash.'

I answered the unspoken question and bent down to take the dish from the oven.

I heard the scrape of a chair on the floor and the sound of footsteps across the room.

'Daddy ...?'

'Goulash is not one of your mother's better dishes. I'll make myself an omelette later on.'

I put the dish on the table and took the lid off. Aromatic steam billowed out. Through the steam I saw Robin begin to push her chair back also.

'Where are you going?'

'I don't like goulash. I'll have an omelette with Daddy.'

'You'll do no such thing. You'll eat the food I've cooked for you, or you'll go to bed. Sit down. Sit down.'

She sat down.

'I don't know what all this nonsense is. Neither of you has ever announced you didn't like goulash before. Have you?'

She didn't say anything.

I scooped some food from the dish and put her plate in front of her.

'Rice?' I asked.

She shook her head.

I put some food on my own plate and sat down.

I picked up my fork and began to eat.

'It's good,' I said. 'I promise you it's good.'

She sat with her hands clasped in her lap.

He had turned on the television in the sitting-room and I could hear the sound of canned laughter.

'Is this a plot of some sort? Would you explain what is going on?'

She stared at her plate.

'Robin!'

'Plot,' she said with contempt. 'Why should I eat goulash if I hate it? If it makes me sick? It makes me sick even to smell it.' She clutched at her throat with a hand. 'I need to be sick.'

'Go ahead,' I said and continued to eat. My hand was shaking as I lifted the fork to my mouth.

She made a retching sound.

'Don't you dare throw up in here.'

'Elizabeth's mother never makes her eat food she doesn't like.'

'Neither do I, as you well know. Now, stop

257

being silly and eat your supper.'

She didn't move, just sat there with her hand still clasping her throat.

I knew I wasn't handling the situation very well.

I ate in silence and she stared at her plate and disembodied voices and laughter floated from the sitting-room.

I wondered if a large gin and tonic would help, but decided it wouldn't.

The goulash was delicious.

I helped myself to some more.

'Have some salad,' I said quite agreeably to her.

She shook her head.

'Well then, you'd better run upstairs and go to bed.'

'I'm hungry,' she said.

'Too bad. You're being very silly, darling. You're getting mixed up in something you don't understand. I don't want to lose my temper with you, but I probably will if you go on like this. Now, for the last time, eat your food or go to bed.'

She pushed her chair back and stood up. Tears were pouring down her cheeks. She ran from the room.

'I hate you.'

She choked the words out as she passed me.

*　　*　　*

258

Tararaboomdeay.

Such silly words always came into my head in times of crisis.

Tararaboomdeay.

I pushed a piece of lettuce around on my plate and listened.

The television had been silenced and I could hear her voice jerking out words instead.

I put the lettuce into my mouth and chewed at it.

I tasted nothing at all.

The sound of chewing and her voice tangled together in my ears.

Tararaboomdeay.

'Star.'

His voice called from the hall.

I got up and went to the door.

He stood there holding her hand in his.

'We're going to the hotel for a meal.'

'I told Robin to go to bed.'

He said nothing.

They turned and walked hand in hand towards the front door.

'Put on your coats. It's cold outside.'

Motherly to the end.

Of course they paid no attention to me.

After I heard the car drive off I rang Bill.

I let the phone ring twice and then I put down the receiver.

What was the point?

What is ever the point in bursting your friends' ears?

259

I went into the sitting-room. The television set was sparkling silently in its corner. I turned it off and sat in the semi dark.

I didn't even feel like dancing.

Tararaboomdeay was all I could think in my head.

I was still sitting there when they came home about an hour and a half later.

Oh God, I thought, I haven't concentrated on this. I have no bloody plan. What will I say?

His key was in the door and I was still sitting there in the half dark.

They came into the hall and he slammed the door behind them.

'Bed, little bird. Run up at once to bed. It's late. You'll be tired tomorrow.'

'Need I have a bath?'

'No. Just go to bed quickly.'

'Will you come up and kiss me good-night?'

'In five minutes.'

She ran up the stairs.

He went into the kitchen and I could hear him getting a glass from the cupboard, pouring himself a drink and then running cold water into the glass. Then he came along the passage and into the sitting-room.

'Oh, there you are.'

I didn't say anything.

'In the dark. As usual.'

'Like Moses when the light went out,' I said.

He walked around the room switching on all the lights and then pulled the curtains tight.

He took a deep drink from the glass and then put it on the mantelpiece.

'I hate the dark.'

He stood for a moment by the fireplace tapping a finger on the mantelpiece.

'Why do you have to behave like this?'

'You'd better go up and say good-night to Robin and tell her to wash her teeth.'

'You come up.'

'No.'

He took another deep drink and left the room.

I listened to the murmur of their voices.

Everything important in my life happens off-stage, I thought. I am the most important person in my life, yet so many things happen that I don't know about, people say things that I can't hear, people make decisions that I am not able to discuss. One day, maybe, I will look in the mirror and I won't see myself there.

Phhhht.

I will not exist.

I smiled at the thought.

'What's funny?'

He was standing in front of me, tall, taller than he had ever made himself before.

'Absolutely nothing.'

'I suppose you're laughing at me. Grinning about me.'

'No.'

He leant down and took hold of my arms and pulled me to my feet. He began to shake me

261

slowly, from side to side, his fingers grinding tight into my arms.

He shook harder and harder, his fingers now almost through the flesh, bruising the bone, his eyes stared into my eyes, flat, grey, without light or spark in them. I tried to wriggle from his grip, but he held me too tight.

'Martyn ... Stop ...' I could hardly get the words out as I had to gasp for breath.

'Don't shout at me. You'll upset the child.'

'Please ...'

'She's still awake.'

My feet went from under me.

He seemed to throw me across the room onto the sofa. I tried to get up, but I was shaking so hard that none of my limbs had the power I needed.

He walked slowly across the room towards me.

'Why do you hate me?'

I shook my head. It was all at that moment that I could do.

He stood above me, his hands tense, slightly curled, ready for anything.

Foolishly I began to cry, not sob or anything like that, just silent tears rolling down my face. I couldn't control my hands enough to wipe away the wetness.

He leant down over me, gripping my shoulders with his hands. I could smell the whisky from his breath.

'Cry. That's what all women do when they're

found out. They cry.' His full weight was pressing down on me. The tears kept flowing out and down my cheeks, over my chin now and down my neck, wetting the collar of my shirt.

'Lies.' He whispered the word into my face. 'Lies pouring out of your eyes.'

'I don't tell you lies.'

He pressed his hands even harder onto my shoulders. I wondered if his weight would crack my collar-bone.

'I have discovered your secrets, so you cry.'

'I don't know what you're talking about. I'm crying because you're hurting me. I'm hurting, Martyn. Do stop.'

'Sssh.'

'Please!'

'If I could reach into your head and pull out all that stuff that's in there, know what I'd do? I'd chuck it all around the place. I'd grind it in the earth. I'd burn it.'

I tried to push his hands away.

'Let me up,' I begged.

'No.'

'I can't breathe properly.'

'I'd burn it.' He almost whispered the words.

He began to stroke the side of my neck with his left thumb. Round and round rubbing the salt tears into my skin. Then he slipped his wet thumb down through the opening of my shirt. Down and down.

'Leave me alone. Let me sit up. Let me

breathe. I don't want this.'

'I don't give a fuck what you want.'

His cold finger grazed my nipple and I shuddered.

He didn't seem to notice. His fingers began to squeeze and pinch.

'What about what I want for a change? I want a wife, not a zombie sitting in a corner crouched over a typewriter. I want a mother for my child. I want more children. I want loyalty, I want your attention, your love. I want you back.'

He had never raised his voice, but it sounded like shouting in my ears.

I pulled at his hands and pushed them away from me and managed to sit up.

'Just leave me alone.'

He put out his hands again towards me.

'Don't touch me. I'm hurting, Martyn. I don't want you to touch me. This is all ... all ...' My head was spinning. I felt if I stood up, I would fall down; I felt I would never stop shaking again.

'We are both being stupid.'

'I am stupid. That's what you mean. That's what you always think, isn't it? I can see contempt every day in your face.'

'Look ... I think we should have some coffee ... something. A pause to gather our thoughts and then talk. I'll ...' I pushed myself up from the sofa and hoped my legs would hold me '... make some coffee.'

'I don't want coffee.'

'I do. I need to clear my head.'

He moved between me and the door.

His hands were stretched out once more, this time barring my way.

I thought for a moment he was going to perform one of his tricks, but this time nothing as benign as a stream of brilliant stones or a bunch of flowers.

'I don't want you to leave this room,' he said.

I went and sat down on the sofa again. The warmth I had left behind there embraced me. My hands stopped shaking.

'Well? Are you thinking of performing one of your tricks on me? Make me disappear, perhaps? Turn into a potted plant? Or perhaps into some other more acceptable person?'

'A poor joke. Not worthy of your great talent.'

'You talk about secrets? I don't even know who you are, for heaven's sake. Or what you do. I can't bear the anxiety of all this un-knowledge.'

'What a fool you are.'

'I thought I was supposed to think that you are the fool.'

'All you have to do is trust me, believe in me, move through life beside me. Is that too much to ask?'

'Yes.'

'Why?'

'I suppose it's not in my nature to be meek. I

suppose I have an insatiable curiosity. I have grown into being the person I am now. I want to be a writer. You keep your nine lives, or however many there are of them, in sealed boxes. You give me no glimpses. I am living with a part of a person. Do they get glimpses of me?'

'Who?'

'The people in those other boxes. The ones who fill your other lives.'

'You talk such rubbish. You break my heart with your rubbish. I have given you everything anyone could ever want and all you do is accuse me of something ... some sort of mysterious double dealing.'

There was a long silence.

I heard Robin's soft steps in the room above and wondered if she had been listening to us.

'I just don't want you to undermine my authority with Robin,' I said at last. 'That's where all this started, isn't it?'

'I have such expectations for her.'

'And you don't think I have. Oh God, Martyn, have a bit of sense. We all have expectations for our children. Dreams. The eternal hope that they will be happy for ever. We have to teach them that they have to live in a world full of other people. They have to rub along.'

'My children will be different.'

'Child,' I said.

He said nothing.

266

'I'm sorry,' I said, after a long silence.

'That's something anyway.'

He sat down beside me and put a hand on my knee.

I could smell the whisky and the rage from him. His hand was soft, long white fingers and neatly cropped nails, like a surgeon, a pianist, conjuror or, bird man of Alcatraz, a saint in a painting by Botticelli. My mind became crowded with long-fingered possibilities.

He had spoken.

I hadn't heard.

He was staring at me.

'Sorry. I didn't hear.'

He took his hand from my knee and stood up.

'It doesn't matter,' he said. 'It is of very little importance. What I say is obviously of very little importance to you. What I feel is obviously of very little importance to you.'

'I'm sorry. My mind just had a little hiccup.'

He looked me up and down.

'You look awful.'

'It hasn't actually been the best couple of hours of my life.'

'Flippant.'

'True, though.'

'What I said, when you weren't giving me your attention, was that we should start again. Be as we were.'

'How can we do that? Circumstances are different. We are different.'

'You are different certainly. Not any longer the woman I married.'

'What exactly do you mean? I can't be twenty-five again. I can't be childless, I can't...'

'You don't want to try.'

'It seems pointless to try to do something that can't possibly work. We can be something else, if not happy young lovers; we can be happy middle-aged partners.'

He laughed.

'Big deal.'

'It's not a bad deal ... at least I don't think it is.'

'It's not what I had in mind.'

'Isn't it worth thinking about?'

'I'm going to have another drink.'

I said nothing.

He went out into the hall and as he opened the door I heard Robin's feet again scurrying across the floor. Weariness pressed me down into the sofa.

Cowards have no dignity.

I realised after some time that it hadn't been Robin's feet that I had heard. He had gone running up the stairs and I could hear him moving now in my room, little steps backwards and forwards, almost running round the room.

I got up and went to the bottom of the stairs and called up to him. 'Martyn! Martyn! What are you doing?'

He didn't answer.

268

I stood there wondering whether to go up or not.

A wind was blowing down the stairs and his feet ran and ran.

I began to run too, up the stairs and across the landing.

The door of my room was open and I could see thousands of what looked like snowflakes dancing and whirling in the wind from the open window.

He was there, running from my desk to the window, tearing paper into tiny shreds and hurling it out into the darkness. The wind blew the flakes back in again and they rose and fell and lifted again before settling on the floor or the bed or the dressing-table, where they stirred and trembled as if they were alive.

I realised what he was up to.

'Jesus Christ, you rotten bloody bastard!'

'You'll wake the child.'

'Rotten, bloody...' As I rushed towards him he picked up QWERTYUIOP and slung it out of the window. I heard the thud as it hit the ground.

'Fucker.'

I sat down on the bed among the scattered scraps of paper.

I picked up a handful and looked at the typewritten words. My words. Now useless scraps of disconnected thought.

A few scraps of paper landed on my knee.

'Rotten fucker.'

I heard him close down the window. At least, I thought, he hadn't thrown me out, after poor old QWERTYUIOP.

I thought of the morning the fox had killed his doves, of the weight of the child in me at that moment, of the footmarks in the snow.

I picked up another handful of paper, but this time I couldn't even see the words, my eyes didn't seem to be working. My heart was beating in my head as well as in my body.

Banging.

All I could hear was the banging.

I put my cold fingers over my ears to try and control the sound.

No use.

Silly woman. Silly, silly, bereaved woman. Silly, silly, silly.

When I could see again, he was standing by the window, his white hand still, on the frame.

Green frame. His white hand, long-fingered hand on the green frame. I saw nothing for a moment but that hand. Disconnected to anything except the window frame.

'Nearly two years,' I said, pushing the pieces of paper from my knees onto the floor. I began to brush the paper from my bed. I knew I couldn't stand up and I didn't want to give him the pleasure of seeing me fall.

I heard the sound of his feet moving through the paper on the floor. 'Is this one of your illusions?' I asked him. 'Can you now wave your hands and put all those shreds back

270

together again?'

I looked up at him, waiting for an answer.

'One wave of your white hands. Have you got my script hidden under a red silk scarf somewhere? Perhaps...'

I stopped speaking. I couldn't think of what to say next.

'Words!' He spoke that word with such contempt. 'All those words. God, how I hate those words you seem to love so much. I would burn books. Know that? I would really burn books if I had that power. You'll get over this.'

'Yes. I suppose I will. Will you go now. I want to tidy up and go to bed.'

'Tomorrow...'

'Tomorrow, I am going home. I will take the child and go home. I don't know why I didn't do it years ago.'

He looked at me for a moment in silence and then began to laugh.

'What a silly Star you are.'

He put his hand out to touch my head, but I jerked away and his hand for a moment stroked the air.

'I love you,' he said.

'Go fuck yourself.'

'I will make you happy again. We will...'

'Get out of this room. I hope you won't be here when I get up. I never want to see you again.'

He moved towards the door.

'You'll calm down.'

271

'Out, Martyn. Get out of this room and close the door. I don't even want to hear you moving around.'

He got out and closed the door.

I got up from the bed and somewhat foolishly began to pick up the pieces of paper, one by one from the floor, from the bed, from the chairs and tables, from the dressing-table. I didn't know what to do with them, so I took a pillowcase off one of my pillows and I stuffed them well down into it and I filled it until it was almost bursting and then I put it standing against the wall and I went and fell onto my bed.

The fragments danced before my eyes all night long, whether I was awake or asleep, it made no difference. The alphabet of my thoughts danced. I couldn't remember anything about the book at all for those few hours, just the whirling combinations of letters, black on white. *'The ... by the t ... how many b ... I see y ... questi...'* They whirled like snowflakes, settled, and as I stooped to pick up a piece or two, they would whirl away, teasing, out of my reach. *Cat ... catc ... catc ... catch ... hahaha ... cat ... come lady ... cry ... run ... qwertyuiop ... Poor bloody old qwertyuiop lying out there on the gravel. Maybe typewriters don't break if dropped from a height.* Maybe they do.

That's for the morning.

Cold light of morning.

Tomorrow's another day. Perhaps even another life.

*　　*　　*

My eyes hurt when I opened them the next day.

Pale, unfriendly light pressed against the window-panes.

I was still in yesterday's clothes.

I hated that.

I hated even more the silence of emptiness when I opened my bedroom door and went out onto the landing. His door was open, his room empty.

Her door was open and her bedclothes were strewn around the floor, as if she had deliberately thrown them there to annoy me.

'What is annoy?' she would have asked years before. These days she knew the answer.

The kitchen was as I had left it the night before; the wilted salad in a blue bowl on the table by my dirty plate, the goulash on top of the cooker and Robin's untouched plate of food at the place where she had been sitting.

A large sheet of white paper was propped against the salad bowl.

Dear Mummy,

I have gone with Daddy.

He says you are going away. He says you want to take me with you. I don't want to go

273

with you. I want to stay here with Daddy and the birds and go to boarding-school in September. I love Daddy very much. Please don't think that you can make me change my mind, because you can't. Robin Glover.

I read it twice and then folded it up and put it in my pocket.

I threw the slimy lettuce into the bin and then scraped the goulash after it. I took the bin from under the sink and went out of the back door and emptied the small bucket into the big dustbin.

This was Thursday, the day the bin men came. I was about to pick up the bin and bring it to the gate when I thought of poor old QWERTYUIOP. I went round to the back of the house to investigate. The typewriter must have landed on one corner as it was now lozenge shaped and most of the keys stuck out like a porcupine's quills.

'You really didn't deserve this,' I said as I picked up the corpse. I carried it back to the dustbin and put it in on top of the rubbish. Then I thought, why the hell should I drag this to the gate? Why the hell?

I slammed the lid down and left it sitting outside the back door.

I made myself some tea and sat and drank it at the table amongst the dirty dishes.

I knew him well enough to know that there was no point in waiting around for them to come home; there was no point in trying to track them down; the only thing to do was get the hell out, so I went up and packed and called a taxi and the last thing I did before leaving the house, leaving the keys neatly and prominently on the hall table, was to take the pillow case into his bedroom and empty all the scraps of paper onto his unmade bed. I didn't think that was too mean and vindictive really.

I got the taxi to take me to Bill's office in Bloomsbury, an extravagant gesture that I couldn't really afford; in fact I had to borrow the money to pay for it from Bill.

'Deduct it from my next advance,' I said.

He put his arms round me and held me tight. He smelled awfully good; I wondered what it was.

'I love you sport,' he said. 'I'll buy us lunch and then I'll drive you to the airport. I presume that's where you want to go?'

I nodded and my eyes began to fill with tears. He handed me a handkerchief.

'Don't cry,' he said, 'or you'll ruin my reputation.'

I laughed a little.

He picked up the telephone.

'Sylvia. Be an angel and cancel all my appointments for today.'

Sylvia said something that I couldn't hear.

'Tell them I've gone to the Frankfurt book fair.'

I heard her laugh.

275

His jokes and his gentleness got me onto the plane without ever having to use his handkerchief.

I handed it back to him as I moved towards the long 'Passengers Only' tunnel.

'Keep it, sport. It may come in handy. And reinvent that book, there's a good girl. Think of how much you owe me for that taxi.'

He hugged me. He kissed me and for a moment I thought that he was going to cry.

'For God's sake, sport. Let's face it, it's only an hour in a plane. Closer than flaming Ipswich. Love ya.'

The words floated down the tunnel after me, as I ran towards my life.

So I came home.

Alone, as I had left.

*   *   *

How strange, I thought as I heaved my suitcase through the green channel and out into the crowded arrival hall, that woman looks like my mother. Maybe I've forgotten what my mother looks like, maybe that is what I want my mother to look like, a comfortable lady in a hat. Benign. A small sigh shuddered around my body, oh God, how I wanted her to be benign.

'There you are dear. The plane is late, as

usual. Do you need a trolley? No point in rupturing something inside. Your father is hovering in the car.'

I put the case down and stared at her.

'Mother ... I ... How? Well hello.'

She held her pale face towards me for a kiss and I threw my arms around her.

'Mother.'

She patted my back.

'Mind my hat,' she said and then touched the side of my face with a finger. 'Now dear, if you're not going to get a trolley, pick up your case. We mustn't keep your father hovering for too long.'

Obediently, I picked up my case.

Everything inside me was rupturing and tears were bubbling into my eyes.

'How ...?'

It was all I could say. I said it to her back as she pushed a way for us through the crowds.

'Your nice friend Bill, dear. He rang. Luckily we were in. Your father cancelled his golf and here we are. Nice friend. Ah, there he is.'

My father had somehow managed to pause just opposite the door, at the head of a taxi rank. A taxi driver was leaning in the window of the car talking to him. My father was smiling, nodding his head.

When he saw us approaching he waved and opened the car door.

'Wonderful,' he said.

The taxi driver discreetly took his elbow as

he got out of the car. Father came round onto the pavement and kissed me.

'Ah, wonderful. Stella. Lucky we were in.'

The taxi driver picked up my case and swung it into the boot.

'Just get into the car, dear, and cry in there,' said my mother.

I nodded and stepped through the door that my father was holding open for me.

'There's Kleenex on the back window,' said my mother.

I wanted to laugh as well as cry, but presumed my mother would prefer it if I cried, so I did. Quite gracefully.

My father shouted his thanks and farewell to the taxi driver and we were off.

'Nice fellow that. He gave me the number of his outfit. You never know when you might need a taxi. A reliable taxi. So you've left that man. You took your time about it, I must say. What about the child ... little ...?'

'Robin,' said my mother.

I shook my head. The tears became a little less graceful.

'She didn't want to come with me.'

'Tttt.'

As he made the sound he whirled out onto the main road and put his foot down.

'Might get nine holes, if we get back in time.' There was a long silence.

'What you need is a good solicitor.'

Then I laughed and my mother laughed too

and my father laughed and we were all pleased that I was home.

*　　　*　　　*

I hear her slow footsteps crossing the hall; dragging steps as if she didn't want to reach her destination.

I suppose I must be her destination, temporary at least.

After a moment's silence the door opens and she comes in.

She stands in the doorway, rubbing at her lip with a finger.

God, but she looks like him, more than I had ever noticed before.

Maybe it's just another illusion; perhaps she is thinking so hard about him that she has willed the patterns of her face to become those of his.

I clear my throat slightly, not wanting to disturb her with crass words.

She nods at me and walks over to the fireplace. She puts herself with her back to me, hands braced on the mantelpiece.

'I like fires,' she says.

Mmmmm.

'Sort of old-fashioned. No one in England has fires any longer. That was Dad's solicitor. Mr Warner. He always calls me Emily. I never think he's talking to me. It's odd.'

She turns round and looks me in the face.

'Star?'

I don't bother correcting her this time. Life is too short.

'Tell me about Dad.'

'I expect you know more than I do. What sort of things do you want to know? Personal memories? Or what? I do have to say I hardly remember what he looked like. What ...?'

'Star.'

I stop waffling and wait.

She clears her throat.

Oh, God help her, I think. What has the bastard done to her?

'Have you ever heard of Angela ... Brambell?'

May I speak to Angela please?

I never knew her name was Brambell.

'Well ... your father had a secretary once called Angela. Angela who or what, I don't know. I think she got married and left some time ago. I don't know. I know very little. I remember she was cheeky to me on the telephone once. I didn't like her much. Your father never talked about the office. I never knew...'

'I know you never knew. You went on and on about it. I'm sorry. I didn't mean that to sound accusatory. Angela has a daughter called Hazel Angela.'

She clears her throat again.

'Hazel Angela Brambell.'

Conversations of this sort take their own time to mature.

A log resettling in the fireplace behind her sounds for a moment like an avalanche, but she doesn't seem to notice.

'He called her Dove.'

'He?'

Silly question, I think.

'Daddy. It's in the will ... Hazel Angela Brambell, known as Dove.'

He always was a fucker.

'She is my sister.'

'Half,' I say.

'She is my sister. He is her father. We are his children.'

'Well ... I suppose after I left...'

Here I go, making excuses for the fucker.

'She is six months younger than I am, Star.'

I have the most appalling desire to laugh, but I keep a strict control over my face, my throat, my lungs from where the laughter seems to be bubbling.

'Darling...'

'Six months. Surely you knew...'

I hold my hand up in front of me wanting to stop some sort of torrent of recrimination.

'She cried at the wedding. That's all I know ... that's all. All I know. We can't have a conversation about this, if you don't believe what I say to you.'

I wait.

I want to put my arms around her and say all sorts of silly things, like it'll be all right, you've got me, but I reckon she has to find that out for herself.

She nods. She gives a small grimace in my direction.

'Was I Mrs Glover, or Mrs someone else, or even Mrs no one at all? I don't suppose it mattered. It certainly doesn't matter now. He was like a cat who lived his nine lives simultaneously. Truly a master of illusion. I always hoped that he would not always lie to you, but I should have known better. Perhaps I should have fought harder. I should have sent more solicitor's letters but I always felt that he would win in the end, that he would make sure you would hate me so much that the whole victory would be ashes in the mouth. I love you, Robin. I'm sorry you've been buggered about like this, but I do have to say that you'll get over it.'

She didn't say a word.

'Perhaps it's a good thing to know the truth.'

'Why?'

'I suppose it's just the way I look at things. If truth exists, it must be important. Tell me darling ... what did the solicitor say?'

'He didn't know anything about it either. He opened this envelope Dad had left with him and there it was, all about ... about ...'

'Hazel Angela Brambell.'

She nods.

'Her ... her date of birth, her address. Married woman of the following address ... and ... mother of my grandchildren. He wrote that and ... he's left her all his money. Maybe he didn't have much ... wouldn't know what he had, but he's left it to her. He says ... he's written down that he spent lots on me when it was necessary and he's ... well ... and a flat in Kensington to Angela.'

She takes a long deep breath.

'Doesn't he mention you?'

'Oh yes. He's left me the house in Suffolk.'

'Heavens,' I say. 'Does he still ... did he still have that? And all those birds, who did he ...?'

'Dr Rhodes.'

'I think I'll get us a drink. Strong.'

I almost run out of the room.

I don't like to close the door behind me but I pull it over ... just in case I do something untoward.

I mix two large gin and tonics, ice cubes and half a slice of lemon each and look up and find her in the kitchen doorway staring at me.

'Clear-cut and unequivocal.'

I hand her a drink.

'You'll get a few bob for the house.'

'It's not the money. You know that for heaven's sake. You're not an ass. It's like being pushed off the top of a swing by your best friend. That's all.'

She takes a long drink.

Her eyes look very shiny.

'Clear-cut and unequivocal. That's what Mr Warner says. No point, he said, in raising hell.'

'I'm glad that Mr Warner has a bit of sense.'

'I have sense, Star.'

'Stella. My name is Stella, Robin, once and for all. Do please stop calling me a name I hate.'

'He didn't even leave me a letter of explanation.'

'He wouldn't. My dear child, even if you'd attended his deathbed he wouldn't have explained anything. He felt no need for explanations but I'm sure he loved you, if that's any help.'

'Thanks, Marjorie Proops.'

She puts her glass down on the table.

'I'm going now.'

'Back to London?'

'Back home. Can you ring me a cab?'

'I can drive you to the airport.'

'No thanks.'

She leaves the room.

Somewhere I have the number of a reliable cab. I've had it a long time.

I remember my mother's hat that day at the airport, and I do believe she was wearing gloves. As I punch out the numbers I wonder would I have been a better mother if I had worn a hat from time to time, and gloves?

The laughter is still there inside me. That makes me feel rotten.

I order the cab.

'Now,' I say. 'Now. As soon as possible.'

Robin comes back into the room with her small bag. She picks up her glass again and gulps it down in one go.

'I don't want to talk about it any more. That's all,' she says.

'That's all right, darling. I understand.'

'Like hell you do.'

'Do remember it's not her fault. It's no one's fault.'

'Dove. Mother. I'll never see her. I don't want to have any ... Mother ...'

I move over to her and put my arms around her.

'Remember the foxes?' I ask.

She shakes her head.

'No. What foxes? Should I remember?'

'No, darling. I just have such a flittery mind, that's all.'

I kiss the side of her face. It is boiling hot.

'Will you be all right?'

'Yes of course. One thing he taught me is to be all right. He was OK really, wasn't he?'

Before I have time to tell a lie the taxi hoots outside in the street.

She jumps away from me, longing to be gone, to be alone in a taxi or on an aeroplane, just anywhere else.

'No,' I say, as we move towards the door. 'He bloody wasn't all right. He made my life misery. He is making your life misery, and I'm sure he made all those Angelas miserable too. So don't fool yourself. Just cure yourself.'

I open the door and she walks out into the garden.

The driver leans from the front of the car and opens the back door.

She doesn't speak.

One day she will speak.

I follow her to the gate.

It is a beautiful evening; the sky the shimmering colour of a peacock's tail with one little sliver of a silver moon hanging over Howth head.

A sliver.

She slams the car door and lifts her hand in farewell as they drive away.

'I love you,' I call after her, but I don't suppose she hears.

I will go into the house now and close the door.

I will close out the peacock evening and the sliver of the moon.

I will dance.

I would like to be able to dance a dance of love and anger and sorrow and then of course hope, but, being the person I am I will probably just tap around the kitchen. 'Puttin' on the Ritz'. 'It's Only a Paper Moon', 'I wanna be loved by you, nobody else will do...'